"What's wrong, Gemma?" Jesse came around the fireplace.

She sat up and drew her knees up under her cloak. "Nothing. I'm fine."

"You use that word far too often. How can you be fine?"

"You have a point. I would love a cup of hot tea and a cracker. Any chance that Dale left some in his toolbox?"

"I'll check. Chamomile or Earl Grey?"

Her eyes widened with surprise. "Jesse Crump has a sense of humor."

"Don't look so amazed." He stoked the fire.

"I noticed it was snowing again while I was on the porch. Heavily. No one will be able to follow our tracks, will they?"

"Nope." At least she understood why help wouldn't be coming.

"So, what do we do?"

"The hardest thing of all in a survival situation. Stay put."

Her eyes grew wide. "When you say survival situation, are you telling me that we are in serious trouble?"

There was a long silence. "*Ja.* We are."

After thirty-five years as a nurse, **Patricia Davids** hung up her stethoscope to become a full-time writer. She enjoys spending her free time visiting her grandchildren, doing some long-overdue yard work and traveling to research her story locations. She resides in Wichita, Kansas. Pat always enjoys hearing from her readers. You can visit her online at patriciadavids.com.

Books by Patricia Davids

Love Inspired

North Country Amish

An Amish Wife for Christmas
Shelter from the Storm

The Amish Bachelors

An Amish Harvest
An Amish Noel
His Amish Teacher
Their Pretend Amish Courtship
Amish Christmas Twins
An Unexpected Amish Romance
His New Amish Family

HQN Books

The Amish of Cedar Grove

The Wish

Visit the Author Profile page at Harlequin.com for more titles.

Shelter from the Storm

Patricia Davids

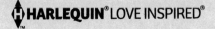
HARLEQUIN® LOVE INSPIRED®

Recycling programs
for this product may
not exist in your area.

 LOVE INSPIRED BOOKS

ISBN-13: 978-1-335-47937-2

Shelter from the Storm

www.Harlequin.com

Printed in U.S.A.

For thou hast been a strength to the poor,
a strength to the needy in his distress,
a refuge from the storm, a shadow from the
heat, when the blast of the terrible ones
is as a storm against the wall.
—*Isaiah* 25:4

This book is dedicated to all the men and women who work in neonatal intensive care units across the country. You care for the least of God's children. May you know abundant peace and joy in your work.

Chapter One

That couldn't be Gemma Lapp.

Jesse Crump turned in his seat to get a better look at the Amish woman on the sidewalk waiting to cross the street. She was wearing a black Amish traveling bonnet and a long dark gray cloak. She was pulling a black wheeled suitcase behind her. He couldn't get a good look at her face. His driver and coworker, Dale Kaufman, pulled ahead when the light changed, and Jesse lost sight of her. There was nothing outward to suggest it was Gemma other than the Amish clothing but something about her, perhaps her small stature, reminded him strongly of the woman he wished he could forget.

"What's the matter?" Dale asked, noticing Jesse staring behind them. "Is something wrong with the load?" He slowed the pickup and trailer carrying two large garden sheds.

Jesse turned around to stare straight ahead. "I thought I saw someone I knew."

"That Amish woman waiting to cross the street?"

Dale knew Gemma. Jesse hoped he had gotten a better look. "*Ja*, did you see who it was?"

"I saw she was Amish by her clothing, but I couldn't see her face because of that big black bonnet. Who did you think it was?"

"Gemma Lapp." He had been thinking about her lately. She was on his mind far too often. Perhaps that was why he imagined he saw her.

Dale glanced his way. "You mean Leroy Lapp's daughter? I thought she was in Florida. Boy, that would be a great place to live during the winter, wouldn't it? Have you ever been there?"

"*Nee.*" Jesse was sorry he'd said anything. Most of the three-hour drive had been made in silence, the way Jesse liked it, but only after Dale tired of Jesse's one-word answers to his almost endless chatter.

Dale accelerated. The ancient truck's gears grated when he shifted. "It could be that she's on her way home for a visit. The bus station in Cleary is just down the block from that corner."

"Maybe."

Dale shook his head. "Nah. Leroy would've mentioned something if she was coming home. That girl is the apple of his eye. She was always easy on the eyes if you ask me. Too bad she got baptized before I had the chance to ask her out."

Jesse scowled at Dale. The man wasn't Amish, but he worked for an Amish bishop. "If you want to keep delivering sheds and supplies for Bishop Schultz, you'd better not let him hear such talk." It was the longest comment Jesse had ever made to the man.

Dale's stunned expression proved he got the point.

"I meant no disrespect, Jesse. I like Gemma. You know how Leroy is always rattling on about her."

Jesse leaned his head back and stared out the window at the homes and small businesses of Cleary, Maine, flashing past. He had eavesdropped on Leroy's conversations about Gemma a few times. He knew about her job in Pinecrest at a pie shop, about the large number of friends she was making among the *Englisch* and Amish folks, and how much she loved the ocean, but he had never asked about her himself.

Bishop Elmer Schultz—like most of the men in their community, including Jesse—had a second occupation, in addition to being a potato farmer. The bishop owned a small business that made storage sheds in various sizes. Jesse had worked for him since coming to Maine three years ago when the community of New Covenant was first founded.

Starting a new Amish colony anywhere was filled with challenges, but the rugged country of northern Maine had its own unique trials. Here, more than anywhere, a man had to depend on the people around him in times of trouble. There was no certainty that the community founded by Elijah Troyer could survive. Elijah had passed away two years ago. Nine of the original ten families remained and more had come the past summer.

The move to New Covenant, Maine, may have been a difficult choice for some of the families in the community, but not for Jesse. He had jumped at the chance. In Maine he didn't have to hang his head because he wasn't as smart as some or because he was bigger than everyone else. In Ohio he'd been known as Jesse the Ox since his school days.

The child of a single mother, he'd been orphaned at

thirteen. He quit school and became a hired man with no hope of owning his own land until he answered an ad in the Amish newspaper seeking hardy souls willing to settle in northern Maine and offering a small parcel of land as an incentive. The beautiful scenery of Maine and plenty of hard work soon overshadowed Jesse's memories of his unhappy early years. Until Gemma Lapp managed to reopen those old wounds with her sharp tongue.

He could still see her standing with her arms crossed and her face flaming red as she sputtered, "Jesse Crump, you're as big as an ox and dumber than a post."

All because he had rebuffed her offer of marriage.

She had barely been twenty-one at the time, not old enough to know what love was, but she'd taken the notion that she was in love with him. He'd suffered through weeks of her attempts to gain his affection. She tried everything from fresh-baked pies delivered to him at work, letters full of her newfound love, even getting her father to hire him to do handiwork on their farm, where she was always close by, chatting about how wonderful it would be to marry and have children.

He was almost eight years her senior and not interested in settling down until he had enough land to support a family. Her proposal wouldn't have been so bad if they had been alone, but they hadn't been. A half dozen people overheard her offer, his pointed rejection and her scathing words in reply.

The snickers, taunts and jeers that had made his school years and young-adult life miserable were only in his head but in that moment, Gemma had unlocked feelings of inferiority he had lived with for years and worked hard to overcome. If she saw him that way, surely others did too.

He kept to himself after that day, hoping her remarks would be forgotten, but they stayed stuck in his head, even though no one else echoed them. He strove to avoid being anywhere near Gemma for the next six months. *Big as an ox and dumber than a post.* It wasn't until she left New Covenant that he stopped hearing her words. In spite of her comment, he hadn't disliked Gemma. She was loyal to her friends. She was a hard worker. She had a good sense of humor, but she was also head-strong and willful.

It had been nearly a year and a half since the embarrassing incident. He thought he'd put it out of his mind, but it seemed he hadn't.

Gemma's father, Leroy Lapp, worked with Jesse at the bishop's business. Leroy had recently been chosen to become the community's second minister. The influx of six new families in the spring had swelled the congregation, making it more than Bishop Schultz and his first minister, Samuel Yoder, could manage. Especially now that plans were underway to start their own Amish school.

"Maybe she's making a surprise visit," Dale said when the silence stretched too long to suit him.

"Maybe you could drive faster. It's almost noon."

"What's your hurry? We've got all day."

"I've got to get back before the bank closes. I need to get a cashier's check for the earnest money the auction company requires I put up before I can bid on the property I've got my eye on. They want ten thousand dollars to prove I can afford the land."

"Oh, right. The land auction. I almost forgot about

that." Dale shot Jesse a sheepish glance and focused his attention on the road.

The farm Jesse owned was small, but he had plans to expand. The money he'd made building sheds over the last few years would help pay for more land. He had his eye on eighty acres that bordered his property to the west. It was fertile land ready for planting in the spring. He couldn't ask for a better piece of property. It was going up for auction the day after tomorrow. The auction company required earnest money in the form of a cashier's check or cash before anyone was allowed to bid and Jesse wasn't about to miss out on the opportunity of a lifetime.

He gazed out the passenger's-side window at the farms that lined the highway, interspersed with heavy forests already covered with the first snow of winter. His thoughts drifted from the land he intended to purchase back to Gemma. If Gemma did come to visit her family in northern Maine, it wouldn't be in the middle of November. Gemma didn't like the snow. To hear her tell it, she didn't like much of anything about Maine.

He was sure his name topped the list of things she disliked most about the North Country.

"There won't be another bus going that way until the day after tomorrow."

"Are you sure?" Gemma stared at the agent behind the counter in stunned disbelief.

The tall thin man with thick glasses stopped writing in a logbook of some sort and peered at her over the top of his glasses. "Of course I'm sure. I work for the bus company."

She held up the flyer she had picked up in Boston. "The schedule said there is a bus going to Caribou every day."

"Look at the small print. There is, until the fifteenth of November. After that, bus service drops to every other day until the fifteenth of April. Today's bus left two hours ago. Won't be another one until the day after tomorrow. Next," he called out, leaning to look around her.

Only one elderly man stood behind her. He held out a piece of white pipe. "Do you have a J-trap that will fit this size and PVC glue?"

"I sure do, but you'll need cleaner, as well." The agent came out from behind the counter and led the man to the plumbing section of the hardware store that doubled as a bus station in Cleary.

Gemma waited impatiently for him to come back. When he did, she clasped her hands together tightly, praying the tears that pricked the back of her eyes wouldn't start flowing. She couldn't afford a motel room for two nights. "I don't have much money with me. Are there any Amish families in this area?"

The man behind the counter rubbed his chin. "Let me think."

The Amish opened their homes to other members of their faith even if they had never met. She would be welcomed, fed and made to feel like one of the family. The command to care for one another was more than a saying. It was a personal commitment taken seriously by every Amish family, no matter how poor or how well-to-do they were. Many times, she had seen her mother stretch a meal for three into a meal for twice that many when Amish travelers appeared unexpectedly at their door. She waited hopefully for the clerk's answer.

He shook his head. "Nope. Not that I'm aware of anyway."

She sniffed as her vision blurred. "Thank—thank you." She started to turn away, humiliated by her runaway emotions. They were one more unhappy part of her horrible situation.

"You might check with the sheriff," the agent offered with a hint of sympathy in his tone. "He may know of some."

She managed a half smile for him. "Where do I find the sheriff?"

"I'll call him for you. He's usually home for lunch at this time of day. You are welcome to wait here." He gestured to a wooden bench sitting in front of a large plate-glass window.

She nodded, unable to speak for the lump in her throat, and wheeled her suitcase over to the bench. Sitting down with a sigh, she moved her suitcase in front of her, so she could prop up her swollen feet. She leaned her head back against the glass and closed her eyes. After two solid days on a bus, she was ready to lie down. Anywhere.

"Miss? Excuse me, miss."

Gemma opened her eyes sometime later to see the agent standing in front of her. She blinked away the fog in her brain. "I'm sorry. I must have fallen asleep."

"You've been snoozing for a couple of hours. The sheriff just got back to me. He's been working an accident out on Wyman Road. He doesn't know of any Amish in these parts. You've been here for quite a while. I thought you might like something to eat. You mentioned you were short on funds, so I brought you a burger from the café down the street." He held out a white paper bag.

"*Danki*. Thank you. That's very kind." She sat up surprised by the unexpected gift. What did he hope to gain by it? She rubbed her stiff neck and waited to hear the catch. "It smells *wunderbar*." She slowly took the bag from him.

"You're welcome to use our phone to call someone. The store will be closing in an hour, but the diner down the street stays open all night." He sent her an apologetic glance and walked away.

She bit her lower lip to stop it from quivering. She could place a call to the phone shanty her parents shared with their Amish neighbors to let them know she was returning and ask her father to send a car for her, but she would have to leave a message. It was unlikely that anyone would check the machine this late in the day.

Besides, any message she left would be overheard. She knew two women who checked the machine each morning for the sole purpose of keeping up with the local gossip. Unless she gave a reason for her abrupt return, speculation would spread quickly. If she gave the real reason, even Jesse Crump would know before she reached home. She couldn't bear that, although she didn't understand why his opinion mattered so much. His stoic face wouldn't reveal his thoughts, but he was sure to gloat when he learned he'd been right about her. He had called her a spoiled baby looking for trouble and said that she would find it sooner or later. Well, she had found it all right. A thousand miles away from him in Florida.

No, she wouldn't call. She didn't want to make her parents the center of conjecture about her return or have them bear the expense of hiring a car to fetch her. What she had to say was better said face-to-face. She was cowardly enough to delay as long as possible. Her appetite gone, she put the burger bag on the bench beside her.

She didn't know how she was going to find the courage to tell her mother and father that she was six months pregnant and Robert Fisher, the man who'd promised to marry her, was long gone.

Jesse and Dale delivered both sheds as promised, but the second customer wasn't ready for them, despite having chosen the date and time for them to arrive. The two men spent an extra three hours helping the owner clear the area where he wanted it. They even leveled out a gravel pad for him before setting the building in place.

Jesse joined Dale in the cab of his ancient but prized pickup when they were done. Dale's expression showed his annoyance. "I can't believe we did all that work for him and then he claimed it was included in the price of the shed instead of paying us. What a rip-off. There are always a few dishonest folks who think they can stick it to the Amish and get away with it, because the Amish won't come after them for the money."

Jesse understood Dale's frustration, but his faith required him to forgive those who would do him ill. "Give thanks that you are not like him. It is better to be a poor man than a dishonest one."

"It's a good thing I'm not Amish. I'm gonna get my money and I'll get yours too. I have a brother-in-law who works for an attorney. I'm not afraid to go after someone who cheats me." Dale turned the truck key but nothing happened. He tried again with the same result. He glanced sheepishly at Jesse. "Don't worry, I've got this."

He hopped out of the cab and reached behind his seat to pull out a large toolbox. "This old heap has taught me to never go anywhere without my tools."

He raised the hood and propped it open, disappearing from Jesse's view. A few seconds later, he looked around at Jesse. "Loose battery cable. Try it now."

Jesse scooted across the bench seat until he was behind the wheel. He turned the key and the truck roared to life. Dale dropped the hood, pushed his toolbox behind the seat again and got in as Jesse moved back to his side of the seat. "Are we heading back, or do you want to get a motel room tonight and start fresh in the morning?"

A glance at Dale's face told Jesse his coworker was worn-out. "We'll get a room."

As eager as Jesse was to get back, making the long drive this late wasn't practical. Tomorrow afternoon would be soon enough to have the bank issue him a cashier's check as earnest money for the auction the following day. He needed the land to expand his farm. It could be years before another piece of farm ground so close to his own came up for sale.

Dale grinned. "Good. Let's get something to eat too."

"Sure." Jesse was getting hungry. The sandwich he'd packed for his lunch was long gone.

"I know this great little burger place just off the highway downtown. Our crew used to eat there every chance we got."

"Crew?" As soon as he asked the question, Jesse knew it was a mistake.

"I worked two summers for a logging company up the way. Didn't I ever tell you that? The pay was good, but the hours were long and the work was dangerous. The first week I was on the job, a tree fell within inches of my head. Inches. That was just the start of it."

Jesse was sure he was about to hear everything that had happened to Dale during those two years. He settled himself in resignation. Hopefully dinner would put a halt to Dale's storytelling.

As they drove back into town, Jesse searched for the Amish woman, hoping to see her face and prove it wasn't Gemma. The streets and sidewalks were almost empty. He didn't spy anyone in Amish clothing. Dale pulled the pickup and empty trailer into a parking lot off the main street. When he opened the door, Jesse got a whiff of mouthwatering fried onions and burgers. If the fare was anything like the aroma, they were in for some good food. His stomach growled in anticipation.

He followed Dale inside the small diner, ducking slightly to keep from knocking his black hat off against the doorjamb. Several people were seated at tables and at a counter. They all turned to look. He should have been used to the stares, but he never got over the feeling that he was an oddity. An Amish giant. At six foot four, he towered over Dale, who was five foot eight at the most. Jesse's hat added another two inches to his height, and his bulky black coat made him look even bigger.

He happily took a seat in a booth where his size was less noticeable. His friend Michael Shetler once told him he needed to hang out with bigger friends. Good advice, but the problem was there wasn't anyone his size in their Amish community.

A waitress came over and pulled a pencil from her dark curly hair. "What can I get you?"

"Two of your lumberjack burgers, two orders of fries and I'll have a soda. What do you want to drink, Jesse?"

"Water."

Dale winked at the waitress and grinned. "The Amish like to keep things simple."

She ignored Dale and focused on Jesse. "Are you with the Amish lady waiting at the bus station? Oscar, the bus station attendant came over a little while ago and bought a burger for her. He said she had missed her bus and didn't have enough money for a motel. She was hoping to find another Amish family in the area. He asked me if I knew any and I don't."

"We aren't from around here," Dale said.

Jesse hesitated a few seconds, then stood up. "Which way is the bus depot?"

She pointed her pencil up the street. "It's not really a depot. The bus line just has a desk in the hardware store."

He touched his hat. "Thank you. Go ahead and eat, Dale." He couldn't leave without offering aid to another member of his faith. He would pay for her motel room and make sure she had money to use for food if she needed help.

He walked out the door and up the sidewalk to the hardware store. A bell tingled as he walked in. A quick glance around showed him a woman in Amish clothing sitting on a bench near the other end of the store. She sat huddled in her seat with her head down and her hands gripping her handbag as if someone might tear it from her grasp.

He stopped a few feet away, searching for something to say, to ask if she was okay, if he could help and he finally settled for a simple "good evening" in the native language of the Amish, Pennsylvania *Deitsh*. *"Guder nacht, frau."*

The woman looked up. He stared at her familiar face in astonishment. "Gemma?"

Her eyes widened. "Jesse?"

The color left her cheeks. She pressed a hand to her lips and burst into tears, leaving him with no idea what to do.

Chapter Two

What was Jesse doing here?

Gemma struggled to control her sobs. He couldn't have looked more stunned if he tried. His expression would have been comical if she could have found anything funny in her humiliating situation. How much worse could this day get?

The bus agent hurried over. He knelt beside her and offered her a box of tissues while glaring at Jesse. "What did you say to her?"

Jesse's face became expressionless. "I said good-evening."

The agent's scowl deepened. "That's not enough to make a woman cry."

"I reckon it is when I say it."

"It's—it's okay," Gemma managed to reassure the helpful man between hiccuping sobs.

She reined in her distress and raised her chin to meet Jesse's gaze. The surprise of seeing him had caught her off guard. His size, as he towered over her, made her feel small and insignificant. Like always. "Hello, Jesse. What—what are you doing here?"

"Delivering sheds. And you?"

She looked away. "Going home. I missed my bus."

He shoved his hands into the pockets of his coat. "Dale Kaufman and I are returning to New Covenant in the morning. You are welcome to ride along with us. I'll get you a room for tonight. Dale's truck is down in front of the café. If you would rather not ride with…us, I'll pay for your room as long as you need one."

He turned and left the building without waiting for her answer. She drew a deep breath and blew it out in a huff. She wanted to get home, but she didn't want to spend hours sitting next to Jesse. Nor did she want to be beholden to him. He had only offered to pay for her room because they were both Amish. He hadn't done it because he cared about her.

Once she had imagined herself in love with Jesse. Was it only a year ago? It seemed like a lifetime had passed. She'd done everything within her power to make him notice her. What he had seen was a pesky child not a woman. Her declaration of love and marriage proposal didn't win her the kiss she'd been hoping for. Jesse had laughed at her and called her a spoiled baby. She'd been humiliated, brokenhearted and furious. She had said some cruel things she didn't mean. As it turned out he'd been right.

She picked up her sandwich bag and lifted the handle of her suitcase. She tried to hand the box of tissues back to the agent.

Her kind protector shook his head. "Keep it. You might need it. You don't have to go with that fellow if you're afraid of him."

That made her smile. "Jesse Crumb might break a foolish young girl's heart, but he wouldn't hurt a fly."

Pulling her suitcase behind her, she left the building and walked toward the café. The autumn wind was cold where it struck her face. It carried the promise of snow. Why people had chosen to settle this land was beyond her. The Florida coast was so much nicer.

Dale Kaufman came out of the building as she approached the vehicle. Jesse was nowhere in sight. Dale grinned. "I sure am surprised to see you, Miss Lapp, and in Cleary of all places. How did you end up here?"

"Cleary is the northern end of the major bus line. I was supposed to take a local bus up to Caribou, but they only run every other day in the winter. One more thing about this state that makes life difficult." She pulled her cloak tightly around her shoulders, making sure to keep the material gathered loosely in front so her pregnancy didn't show.

"So why come back?" Jesse asked as he walked up behind her.

"That's none of your business." She made her tone as sharp as possible. The last thing she wanted him to think was that she still had a crush on him. She'd gotten over him a long time ago. Well before she met her baby's father, she had realized her infatuation with Jesse had been more about being the last single woman in her group of friends than finding her soul mate. There had been only two single Amish fellows in their community back then. In her opinion, Jesse had been the better choice.

He arched one eyebrow but didn't say anything. That was Jesse's biggest problem. He never had much to say. Especially to her. How could she ever have considered him attractive? Sure, he was tall with broad shoulders, curly black hair and the most beautiful sky blue eyes fringed with thick dark lashes, but looks weren't everything. An attractive man needed an attractive personality. Jesse had the personality of a fence post.

No, she was being childish again. Just because he hadn't been blinded by her charms last year was no reason for unkind thoughts about him. Jesse was a quiet man and there wasn't anything wrong with that. He was about the only man she knew who didn't have a hidden motive.

Robert Fisher, her former boyfriend had been a handsome smooth-talking flirt. She had been a naive, easy target for him. His attentions soothed her wounded pride and made her feel beautiful and loved. Except it was all a lie. He seduced her and left town the day after she told him she was pregnant. Like a fool, she had waited for him to return. It took months for her to accept that he wasn't coming back. It was a lesson she took to heart. He was the last man she would trust unconditionally.

Returning home was hard. She had already been baptized into the Amish faith. She would be shunned when the bishop learned of her condition, but that wasn't as frightening as having a baby alone. She wouldn't be able to eat at the same table as her parents and they wouldn't be able to accept anything from her hand. She wouldn't be included in church activities for as long as her shunning went on. She was prepared for that. She fully intended to confess and ask forgiveness and pray the bishop chose a short period of shunning for her to endure.

Jesse held out a motel key. "I got you a room. Number eight. I'll take your suitcase." One arched eyebrow dared her to reject his offer.

"Danki," she murmured.

Dale glanced between the two of them. "Have you eaten, miss?"

She raised the white paper bag. "I have my supper."

"Goot." Jesse walked toward the motel, carrying her suitcase as easily as if it were empty instead of packed full of all she owned.

She nodded to Dale. "I'm grateful for the lift home."

"My pleasure. It's a long trip, and I sure will enjoy having someone to talk to for a change. Jesse don't say much."

"I know." She followed Jesse to the room at the very end of a motel that had seen better days. The Gray Goose Inn's paint was peeling in multiple spots and the windows were dingy. The sidewalk along the front was cracked and lifted while the neon light on the sign out front flickered dimly.

He held open the door and set her suitcase inside. "We'll leave at six."

"I'll be ready." She swallowed her false pride and stared at her fingers clenched around her purse handle. *"Danki,* Jesse. This is generous of you. I will repay you, I promise."

"It's nothing. Why come back? Your *daed* says you like it in Florida."

Had Jesse asked about her? She found that hard to believe. "I do, but I got homesick."

As soon as she said the words, she realized they were true. She missed her parents and her friends, even if they didn't miss her.

Bethany, Gemma's closest friend, had married last winter and all she talked about was how happy she and Michael were and how blessed she was to have found the man God had intended to be her husband. Gemma's first cousin Anna Miller was the same way. She and her new husband, Tobias, had arrived in New Covenant a few weeks after Bethany's wedding. The two women had nothing on their minds except setting up house and starting a family. Two more young married couples moved to New Covenant at the same time. The women all enjoyed one another's company and often visited between houses. Gemma was the only single woman among them.

Gemma had been happy for her friends, but it hadn't taken long to realize she'd become a third wheel. The sad odd person out with no one of her own. Without the prospect of marriage and the memory of making a fool of herself over Jesse popping up each time she saw him, Gemma decided to escape to the Amish settlement in sunny Pinecrest, Florida, to find her own soul mate. What a mistake that had turned out to be. A shudder coursed through her at the memory of her betrayal by the man she had met down there who claimed to love her.

"Are you back for good?" Jesse asked. Was there a hopeful note in his voice? She glanced at his face. His grim expression said she must have been mistaken.

She looked down and shrugged. "I haven't decided."

Her lower lip quivered. The council of her mother was what she wanted and needed, even as she dreaded revealing her condition. She had no idea what she was going to do about the baby.

Jesse stood as if waiting for something else. She glanced at his face again and caught a look of tenderness before it disappeared. His usual blank expression took its place. Underneath his brawny build and his reclusive nature, Jesse had a soft heart. While he avoided the company of most people, he was known for taking in wounded creatures and strays. Was that how he saw her now? If so, he was more astute than she gave him credit for. She glanced down to make sure her full cloak hid her figure. "Thank you again for your kindness."

"The bishop would expect it of me. Gemma, is something wrong?"

She couldn't look at him. "I'm tired, that's all."

"Then I'll say good-night."

Unable to reply, she went inside, dropped her cold supper in the trash and closed the door, shutting out his overwhelming presence and her irrational desire to bury her face against his chest and give in to her tears.

It was still dark when Gemma left the motel room a few minutes before six o'clock the next morning, pulling her suitcase behind her. She could see her breath in the chilly air. Snowflakes drifted gently down from the overcast sky. Winter was tightening its grip on the countryside. The contrast between the sandy beach and ocean waves where she had been three days ago caused her to shiver. Had she been foolish to come back? Maybe.

She had her emotions well under control for the moment. A good night's sleep had erased the ravages of the tears she'd cried into her pillow after Jesse left her. Washing her face with cold water had removed the last bit of puffiness from around her eyes. She was ready to face a few hours in Jesse's company.

He was standing beside Dale's battered yellow pickup waiting for her. Without a word, he took her bag and stowed it in the bed of the truck and held the door open for her. She got in. He climbed in after her, taking up more than his share of the bench seat. She scooted farther away.

Dale got in and handed her two white paper bags identical to the one the bus agent had given her. "I got some breakfast burritos for us to eat on the road." The aroma of toasted tortillas, sausage, grilled peppers and onions filled the air in the small cab, making her stomach rumble ominously. Her morning sickness was more like any-time-of-the-day sickness. It struck without warning. She handed one of the bags to Jesse and swallowed hard, hoping she wouldn't get sick.

Dale kept up a steady line of chatter as he drove northward on the highway. Jesse ate his meal in silence. He took a swig from a bottle of water, recapped it and put it back in the bag. "Aren't you going to eat yours?" Jesse nodded toward the paper sack on her lap.

"I'm not hungry. You are welcome to it."

"Danki." He took the offered bag and finished off her burrito.

Dale chuckled. "He's a big man with a big appetite. It must cost a fortune to keep him fed. No wonder he hasn't found a wife. The poor woman would never get out of the kitchen."

The heat of a blush rose up her neck and across her cheeks. She cast a covert glance at Jesse. He was staring straight ahead. A muscle twitched in his clenched jaw. He hadn't forgotten their last conversation.

After weeks of dropping hints about her feelings for Jesse and her desire to get married, she had finally confronted him point-blank and proposed marriage with disastrous consequences. He'd laughed at her and told her to go home. She had countered by confessing her love and throwing herself into his arms. He'd abruptly put her aside. The scowl on his face and his words still echoed in her mind.

You're not in love with me. You're a foolish, spoiled baby looking for trouble. One day you will find it unless you learn humility.

She wasn't proud of her reaction. She said things she hadn't meant, but she was sure Jesse had meant what he said. He'd walked away, shaking his head, leaving her crushed and fuming. Her humiliation had been complete when she learned some of her friends had overheard their conversation. Her parents had been appalled as the gossip quickly spread. Rather than face it down, after a few months she had packed up and moved to Florida to start a new life.

The sad part was that she really had liked Jesse. It was knowing that he had been disgusted by her behavior that hurt the most.

She dared a glance at him, but his attention was focused out the passenger's side window. She clutched the front of her cloak and sat quietly beside him as Dale chatted away about his ex-wife and her poor cooking.

About thirty minutes into their trip, it began snowing heavily. Fat flakes smashed themselves against the windshield and were swept away by the wipers. As the snow became thicker, Dale grew quieter and concentrated on his driving.

Ahead of them were several semi–tractor trailers. Dale hung back to keep out of their spray. Suddenly the last truck in line went into a skid on the bridge ahead. The rig jackknifed and clipped the rear end of the truck in front of it as it tipped over. The sound of screeching metal reached her as both trucks hit the sides of the bridge. Dale maneuvered his pickup off to the side of the road. Both men got out. Gemma saw the flickering of flames through the windshield that was being quickly covered with snow.

Jesse paused to look at her. "Stay put." He slammed the door shut and jogged away with Dale into the snow.

Gemma had no idea how long she sat in the truck. She prayed silently for all the people involved. The sirens of rescue vehicles announced their arrival before they pulled up alongside her. With police and firefighters on the scene, Dale and Jesse finally returned to the vehicle.

"Is everyone all right?" she asked Jesse as he opened his door.

"Both drivers survived."

Dale knocked the snow off his boots before climbing in behind the wheel. "That is a mess. The bridge will be closed for hours yet. You should've seen Jesse pull the door open on that tipped-over cab and lift that fellow out. If it weren't for him, that guy would be toast."

Jesse stared straight at her. "Sometimes it pays to be as big as an ox."

She didn't know how to reply. He continued to stare at her for a few more seconds, then he looked away. She was left with the feeling that her long-ago comment had hurt his feelings. Had it? She'd only been concerned about her own humiliation at the time.

Not that it mattered. Once news of her condition got out, he would be eternally grateful he had avoided her bumbling advances.

Jesse stared straight ahead. He had given Gemma the opportunity to apologize for her painful comments about him. Either she still believed he was big and dumb or she didn't care about his feelings. She once claimed to love him. If she still harbored tender feelings for him, she was hiding it well. His Amish faith demanded that he forgive anyone who had wounded him. He thought he had done so, but having her so close beside him proved some of his resentment remained.

He had been taunted and ridiculed about his size since his school days. He wasn't the smartest kid in the class, and he knew it. That only made him try harder. He endured the teasing until one day in the fourth grade he hit his antagonist in the face. Wayne Beachy had ended up with a broken jaw. Filled with remorse, Jesse never allowed his temper to take control again. Enduring teasing was far less traumatic than seeing the results of what his fists could do.

That was why his continued resentment of Gemma Lapp troubled him and why she was never far from his thoughts. He didn't understand his reaction. He only knew she made him uncomfortably aware of his size and his lack of intelligence. Gemma was tiny compared to him. Her sharp wit had made her a favorite among the young people in New Covenant. It was only after her best friend, Bethany, married Michael Shetler that her wit took on a cutting edge.

He should've been glad when she decided to move to Florida, but he hadn't been. For some unknown reason, he had missed her.

She looked at Dale. "What now? Do we wait here, or do we go back to Cleary?"

"I might have a third option."

"What?" Jesse asked. He had to get to his bank before the close of business today.

Dale half turned in his seat to face them. "You remember that I told you I used to work for a logging company in this area?"

Jesse nodded. "I remember."

"About two miles back, there is a logging road that cuts off this highway and goes about twenty miles back into the hills. It comes out on this same highway about twenty-five miles up ahead. I figure it'll be rough in places, but we'll lose less than two hours of time, which will be better than sitting here waiting for the bridge to be cleared. What do you think?"

"What about the weather?" Jesse asked.

"The snow is letting up. We'll stay ahead of it."

"I say go for it," Gemma said. Clearly the last thing she wanted to do was spend more time than necessary with him.

"What do you say, Jesse?" Dale asked.

"I've got to get home by this afternoon."

Dale grinned and turned the pickup around. "All right, folks. We are about to see some fabulous Maine backcountry wilderness."

Dale had been right. Not about the weather, the snow continued, but about the beautiful scenery and the road being rough. It was more of a trail than an actual road. As they bounced along the narrow track through towering pine trees, Jesse and Gemma were constantly tossed against each other. He had been in many uncomfortable situations in his life but none as uncomfortable as trying to remain indifferent to the little woman continually apologizing for jamming her elbow or her shoulder into his side.

She wasn't doing it on purpose, but that didn't make it any more comfortable. He was tempted to slip his arm around her and pull her tight against him, but he didn't. She might think he was trying to take advantage of the situation.

They reached a more open area, and Dale picked up speed. Suddenly, a bull moose galloped out into the road directly in front of them. Dale swerved. Jesse threw his arm across Gemma as he braced for the impact. The moose sprang forward at the last second. Dale missed him but lost control of the pickup and careened into the trees. The front wheels hit a large fallen log and stopped abruptly, throwing them all forward. Gemma slipped from under Jesse's arm and cried out as she hit the floorboard.

After a few seconds of stunned silence, Jesse pushed himself away from the dash and back onto the seat. "Gemma, are you hurt?"

She had ended up in a crumpled heap on the floor. Dale was slumped behind the steering wheel.

Gemma looked up at Jesse with pain-filled eyes. "Something's wrong with my ankle. I think it may be broken." She tried to lever herself up. He stopped her with a hand to her shoulder.

"Are you hurt anywhere else?"

"Give me a minute." She flexed her neck, shrugged her shoulders, then opened and closed her hands. She shut her eyes and pressed a hand to her midsection.

"What is it?" he asked, concerned by her stillness.

Sighing, she held out a hand. "It's just my left foot. Help me up."

"How bad is it?" He lifted her gently to the seat. The movement caused her to grit her teeth as a deep frown creased her brow.

"Bad enough, but I think I'll live. Are you okay?"

"A few bumps and bruises." His right arm hurt where he had braced it against the dashboard, but it was likely a strain and nothing more. He was a little surprised she had asked.

Turning to the driver, Gemma touched his shoulder. "Dale? Dale, are you okay?"

He moaned and sat back, raising a shaky hand to his head. "I'll get back to you on that. What happened?"

Jesse rubbed his shoulder. "The good news is you missed the moose. The bad news is that you struck something else." The front end of the truck was tilted up at a fifteen-degree angle.

"Anybody hurt?" Dale blinked rapidly as he tried to focus.

"Gemma thinks her foot is broken. I'm fine. How about you?"

"Other than an aching noggin, I think I'm okay." He pushed open his door and looked down. "Wow. This is not good."

Chapter Three

Dale turned off the vehicle, got out and squatted to look under it. His expression told Jesse he wasn't happy with what he saw. Jesse had to force open his door to get out by hitting it with his aching shoulder several times. Gemma stayed put. Her foot had twisted under her awkwardly when she was thrown to the floor. Jesse's arm had kept her face from smashing into the dashboard.

Jesse and Dale conferred outside. Dale took out his cell phone and held it up, turning from side to side. He slipped it back into his pocket and came to the open driver's-side door. "Do you think you can walk, Gemma?"

She shook her head, turned sideways and lifted her legs onto the seat. Her right ankle was twice as big as her left one. She peeled down her stocking and hissed at the pain. Her ankle was already turning black-and-blue. "I doubt I can stand on it, let alone walk."

Dale scooped up a handful of snow and held it against the bump on his head. "This truck isn't going anywhere. The front tire has busted loose, and the body is high centered on a boulder. It's going to take a tow truck to lift it off. The problem is, I don't have phone service in this spot."

"What are we going to do?" Gemma looked around them at the thick forest.

"We're gonna have to hoof it to where I can get cell service and call for a tow truck. Maybe we can fix a crutch for you."

She shook her head. "I'll wait here. Even hobbling, I'd only slow you down."

Jesse glanced from Dale to Gemma and back to Dale. "I don't think we should leave her by herself. I could go, and you could stay here."

Her eyes widened, and she gave a tiny shake of her head. "I'll be fine alone for a few hours." Her smile was half-hearted at best.

He pulled a large blue handkerchief from his pocket, packed it full of snow and handed it to her. "Put this on your ankle. It will help the pain and swelling."

"Danki." She took the compress from him and placed it around her lower leg.

Jesse turned to Dale. "I'll stay with her. Are you sure you are up to the hike?"

Dale managed a lopsided grin. "Fortunately, I have a hard head and my legs are fine." He blinked hard as he stared at his watch. "It's only a little after nine. I don't think we drove much more than ten miles, do you?"

"If that far."

"Even if I have to walk all the way to the highway to get service, which I know I won't have to do, I should still get back with some help before two o'clock."

"We'll be fine." Jesse tried to decide which would be more uncomfortable, waiting in the cold for Dale's return or sitting beside Gemma in the truck for an unknown number of hours.

Dale reached under the seat and pulled out a moth-eaten green army surplus blanket. "This should help keep you a little warmer." He shook it out and handed it to Gemma. She spread it over her legs. Her thin socks and low-cut walking shoes were suited for winter in Florida, not for winter in Maine.

Jesse looked up at the sky. "At least the snow has stopped."

"For now," Dale said. The men exchanged worried glances. They had watched the local forecast on the TV before leaving the motel. They were calling for more snow and the possibility of a blizzard in the coming days.

"Is it safe for you to walk? What if you get lost?" Gemma asked and nibbled at the corner of her lip.

Dale winked. "I'll be fine. All I have to do is follow the tire tracks back the way we came."

Dale sent a speaking glance to Jesse and jerked his head toward the rear of the vehicle. The men walked to the back of the truck to converse out of earshot. Dale pulled his gloves from his pocket and put them on. "It's going to get real cold for her just sitting. Use the heater for fifteen or twenty minutes at a time. The truck has enough gas to run all day if you don't waste it."

"Right. I'll take care of her."

Dale patted Jesse on the shoulder. "I know you will. What I'm saying is, get her talking. That way she'll have less time to worry about her situation. Women need more reassurance when things go wrong."

That hadn't been Jesse's experience. The women he

knew handled the unexpected as well if not better than most men. "I'll do my best."

"Make sure to keep the muffler clear of snow when you run the truck. I don't want to come back and find you passed out from carbon monoxide poisoning or, worse yet, dead."

"I know what to do."

"Okay, see you soon." Dale staggered a few steps before Jesse caught up and steadied him.

"Maybe I should be the one to go."

"I'm fine. You know as well as I do that the bishop and her father would much rather a fine, upstanding Amish fellow stayed with her instead of a not-so-upstanding non-Amish guy like me."

He was right, but Jesse hated to admit it. "Okay, go."

Jesse watched Dale as he walked off until he was out of sight, then he returned to the pickup, praying Dale could make good time in getting them help.

Gemma pulled her cloak tightly around her shoulders. It was growing colder. She studied Jesse's face as he got in the truck beside her. "You look concerned. Are you worried about Dale?"

"I'm sure he will be fine. *Gott* is watching over him." He tried to make his words sound encouraging, but he missed the mark.

It was clear he was concerned for his friend. She could only offer him small comfort. "You're right. I can pray for him, even if I can't do much else."

Jesse nodded to her foot. "How is the ankle?"

"It hurts, but I will be fine here. If you hurry, you can catch up with Dale. I know you'd rather go with him."

"Can you turn on the heater?"

She lifted her chin. "Of course I can."

"Do it."

She stared at the unfamiliar array of gages and knobs until she found the word *heat*. She pushed the slide over, but nothing happened. She glanced at him sheepishly. "Okay, how does it work?"

"The truck has to be running."

"That means turn the key, right?"

He nodded. She grimaced as she scooted behind the wheel and turned the key. Nothing happened. "What am I doing wrong?"

"Probably a loose battery wire." Getting out, he moved to the front of the vehicle and lifted the hood.

"I'd like to know how he expected me to figure that out," she muttered. How often did battery cables come loose?

After a few minutes, he stepped to the side. "Try it now," he called out.

She did, and the engine roared to life, startling her. She pushed the slide over to High. The air came blasting out of the vents. Jesse walked up to the open passenger's-side door. She turned the knob the other way and the flow of air died down. She looked at him, knowing he was testing her, and she was failing miserably. "It's just blowing cold air."

"The engine has to warm up."

Annoyed that she was looking foolish at every turn, she glared at him. "You could've told me that."

"You could have admitted that you don't know anything about running a truck. Did you realize that you have to keep the exhaust pipe free of snow or you will die of carbon monoxide poisoning inside the cab?"

"I didn't. You just love rubbing my face in my ignorance, don't you?"

"That's not true. Can you say the same?" He slammed the door shut and walked to the rear of the vehicle.

Gemma's irritation quickly gave way to guilt. She was in the wrong. She would have to apologize. She shouldn't have snapped at him. Nothing was simple anymore. Every step she took pushed him away, when that wasn't what she wanted. She moved until she was sitting with her back against the driver's-side door and stretched her legs across the seat. In the side mirror, she saw Jesse kick a clump of snow away from the rear tire. He was angry with her.

Why was it that they couldn't have a civil conversation? They were going to be alone together for hours. She watched him pace across the trail behind them with his arms crossed over his chest. She could see his breath rising in white puffs. The snow had started falling again. She couldn't expect him to stay out in the cold while she enjoyed the warmth of the truck. It was clear she was going to have to make the first move. She folded her hands across her abdomen.

She had abysmal judgment where men were concerned. Robert was a prime example. He'd spoken about love and marriage, but he'd used her and cast her aside as soon as she gave in. She betrayed the vows she had made at her baptism and lost her self-respect for nothing.

Love and marriage were out of the picture now. She was about to become an unwed mother. Someone to be pitied. To be talked about in hushed tones, pointed out as an example of what could happen to girls should they stray. She wanted to bury her face in her hands and cry.

Tears slipped down her cheeks, but she scrubbed them away. They solved nothing, but she couldn't stem the rising tide of her remorse.

When Jesse had his anger under control, he glanced at the truck. Gemma's head was bowed and her shoulders were shaking. Was she laughing at him? He'd been the brunt of her teasing before. He'd give a lot to know what she found funny in their current situation. As he walked past the truck bed, he caught the smell of gasoline. Leaning down, he checked under the truck but couldn't see anything wrong. The undercarriage was resting on a snowdrift but the smell of gas was stronger. He wished he knew more about trucks, but he knew enough to be sure it was dangerous to run the vehicle if the gas tank was leaking.

He pulled open the cab door. Gemma wasn't laughing. She was weeping. His anger evaporated. "I'm sorry, Gemma. Don't cry."

"I can—can cry if I—I want to." She wouldn't look at him as she sniffed and wiped her nose with a tissue from the box on the dash.

"We need to turn the truck off. It's leaking gas."

Her eyes widened. She quickly turned the key and the engine died. "Is it dangerous?"

"Not unless something sparks. We'll have to get by without the heater. I'm sorry I hurt your feelings. Please forgive me."

"I'm crying because my ankle hurts."

He sighed heavily. "Then I'm sorry I made your ankle hurt worse."

"Go away," she snapped and sniffed again. He took a step back. She looked up and held out her hand. "I didn't mean that, Jesse. Don't go. Get in here where it's warm. You'll catch your death out there."

"I'm pretty tough. A day in the cold is nothing new for me."

"Please?"

He got in the truck, gently lifted her injured leg and placed her foot on his thigh. "You should keep it elevated. Is the snow pack helping? Am I forgiven?"

She bent her other knee and scooted forward an inch to make her position more comfortable. "It's hard to be upset with someone who is being kind." She rubbed both eyes with her hands.

"I will make it a point to be kind more often. I think we should get your shoe off, but that is up to you."

She bit her bottom lip and nodded. "I'm already crying. I guess now is as good a time as any."

She braced herself, but he was incredibly gentle as he pulled her shoe off her swollen foot. It immediately relieved some of her pain. He placed her shoe and sock on the dash and settled her foot on his leg again. "It needs to be taped up."

"With what?"

He opened the glove compartment and pulled out a roll of duct tape he had noticed yesterday. "This might work. I'll need to put your sock back on. I don't want to plaster this to your skin."

After a few minutes, he had fashioned a crude brace for her foot. "How is that?"

"Okay. Better I think."

"Warm enough?"

"The blanket helps."

"I don't know how. It has more holes in it than a

cheese grater." He reached over, tucked it tightly around her shoulders.

"How long do you think it will take Dale to get help?"

"It's hard to say. Four hours, maybe less."

She leaned her head back against the glass and untied the ribbons of her bonnet. "Then we won't be rescued anytime soon."

"You might as well try to get some rest."

Far from sleepy, Gemma closed her eyes anyway, but she could feel his gaze on her face. She endured it as iong as she could. She opened one eye. "What are you staring at?"

"I was trying to figure out what is different about you."

"I've got a suntan. The sun actually shines during the winter in Florida, unlike this place, which is dreary from late September until May."

"You think these beautiful snow-covered pines are dreary?"

"I do."

She could see he was disappointed with her answer. If he thought the snow-covered woods and gray skies were beautiful, then he was odder than she had imagined. She waited for his next comment. She had never had this much of a conversation with him before. When he didn't say anything else, she closed her eyes but her throbbing foot allowed her to sleep only fitfully. Sometime later, the cold roused her. She raised her head and found Jesse rubbing the frost off a spot to see out.

"Are they here?" she asked hopefully.

"Not yet."

"Oh." She leaned back and pulled the blanket up

around her shoulders. "Can we have the heat on for a while?"

"I don't think we should risk it."

"Not even for ten minutes?"

He shook his head. "I checked the gas gauge a half hour ago and the tank is almost empty. I know Dale filled up this morning before we left the motel. If the gasoline has pooled under the truck, we could start a fire. Or worse."

"Worse?"

"An explosion."

That would be worse, she conceded silently. He knew more about vehicles that she did. She was cold, but she trusted his judgment and didn't push the issue. "It's snowing again."

It wasn't a question. The windshield was covered. He moved her foot off his lap and opened his door. "I'm going to check the trail for any sign of them."

"That seems silly. You can't see much outside and you'll only get colder."

"Moving around will help me warm up."

"Oh, okay. That makes sense. I wish I could join you."

A gust of wind blew in the snow as he got out. It settled on her blanket and sparkled in the dome light. He closed the door and she shivered. She might not be able to walk but she could still move. She spent the next few minutes swinging her arms as she bent and straightened her good leg. It helped a little.

Relief surged through her when Jesse opened the door again. She hadn't realized how safe his presence made her feel. "Anything?"

"Nothing."

"They should be here soon, shouldn't they?" She waited for his reassurance.

"The snow will slow them down. The wind is picking up out there too. Parts of the road could be drifted over by now."

A chill slid over her skin that had nothing to do with the temperature. "They will still be able to reach us, right?"

Chapter Four

Dale should've been back by now. Something must have gone wrong.

Jesse didn't say that to Gemma. He had scanned the trail behind them for any sign of movement or the sound of another vehicle approaching. There was nothing but the wind in the trees and the snow flurries that continued to worsen.

It was past two o'clock and the temperature was dropping. He had to make a decision and soon. The first rule when stranded in the wilderness was to stay put, but he had to get back to New Covenant tonight or lose his chance to purchase the land he wanted. The bank would open at eight in the morning. The auction was set to begin at nine o'clock. He could still turn over the earnest money before the bidding started as long as he made it home tonight and got to the bank as soon as it opened.

"Any number of things could have slowed Dale down. We might have to head back soon," he said.

Without gas, he couldn't run the truck's heater. While the cab gave them protection from the wind and snow, without heat, it would be like staying inside a cold tin can. The forecast that morning had called for temperatures to drop to near ten degrees. It was going to get very cold tonight.

"What do you mean by heading back?"

"What I said. Don't worry about it."

"You need to work on your communication skills." She scowled at him but fell silent, and he was grateful. He got out before she could grill him.

Another ten minutes passed. The visibility dropped to fifty yards as the snow moved in. He would have to go now while he still had a trail to follow. If Dale had reached help and someone was coming, they would meet each other on the road. If for some reason he hadn't made it, Jesse could still get Gemma back to civilization before dark and get to New Covenant before morning.

She was a small woman, but he doubted he could carry her all the way to the highway. He needed a sled and he saw only one option. Dale wasn't going to like it.

Jesse walked to the truck and opened the driver's side door. Even huddled in the blanket, he saw Gemma shiver. She looked at him hopefully. "Is Dale back?"

"Nee."

"What are you doing?"

"Taking us out of here." He closed the door.

He was amazed at the number of tools Dale had crammed into his battered metal toolbox. There was even a short-handled ax, which had dozens of uses in the wilderness. He quickly removed the bolts that secured the hood to the vehicle. With it free, he tipped the curved hood onto the snow and pushed it back and forth. The rounded edges at the front made it a perfect sled. He fashioned a harness from the tie-down straps to go over each shoulder.

Gemma had rolled down the window and was watching him. She wore a wary expression. "Let me rephrase my question. What are you making?"

"A sled."

"For me to ride on?"

"That's right."

"Will you fetch my suitcase for me?"

He shook his head. They were running out of time. "I'd rather we left it here. That way I don't have to pull unneeded weight."

"I understand, but there are some things I need from it before we go."

He shrugged and grabbed it out of the back. She opened the door and took it from him. *"Danki."*

He stood for a few minutes trying to decide the best way to cushion Gemma's ride. Sitting directly on the cold metal would quickly make her uncomfortable. What he needed was a couple of quilts. Lacking those, he decided a cushion of pine boughs might do the trick. Taking Dale's ax, he walked into the woods looking for a young white pine. Their needles were soft and flexible. He found what he was looking for and brought back an armload. He dumped it onto the overturned truck hood. It was about the best he could do for her.

He stepped up to the truck door. "We should get going. I want to reach the highway before dark."

"I'm almost ready."

She had her back to him. She had taken off her cloak and put on two more dresses over the one she wore. She looked as plump as the bishop's wife. She put a second *kapp* over the one she was wearing and then tied her traveling bonnet over both. "Without warmer clothes, layering is the next best thing. I'm afraid I'm wearing most of the extra weight you were concerned about pulling."

"Don't worry about that. It's a *goot* idea." He was surprised she'd thought of it. "Do you have any gloves or mittens?"

She lifted a pair of socks from the seat beside her. "These will work as mittens."

"Okay. Are you ready?"

She nodded. "As soon as I put on my cloak. We should take the water bottles with us." She grabbed the plastic containers from the dash. One bottle was half-empty. The other one was full. She scooted across the seat toward him and gathered the wadded blanket to her chest.

He rubbed his gloved hands on his trouser legs. He was going to have to pick her up and carry her due to her injured ankle. He knew she understood that without him saying anything because her cheeks were already bright red. He could tell his face was a similar color. He had never held a woman in his arms. That Gemma was the first one made him doubly uncomfortable.

He slipped an arm under her knees and around her back. She curved one arm around his neck as she held the water bottles and blanket with her other hand. He lifted her out of the truck and held her against his chest. She barely weighed anything. He never imagined holding her would feel so amazing, so comfortable.

Speechless, he stood gazing at her face framed by her dark bonnet. Freckles he had never noticed before dotted her nose and cheeks. Had the Florida sunshine made them more noticeable? Her eyes remained downcast. She smelled fresh, like sun-dried linen and faintly of flowers and coconut. It had to be the shampoo she used because Amish women did not wear perfume of any kind. He wanted her to look at him. To know what she was thinking. His feet refused to move.

A gust of wind made her turn her face into his shoulder to avoid the driving snow. The desire to hold her closer and protect her from anything that threatened her surprised him.

"Are you sure this is a *goot* idea?" she asked.

"Maybe, maybe not."

He quickly realized holding her in his arms for any reason wasn't a good one for him. Emotions he'd worked hard to keep hidden were stirring just below the surface. Gemma was not the sort of woman he could care for seriously. She was flighty, and she rattled his thinking.

The wind dropped away. She raised her face to gaze at him. Her luminous green eyes, fringed with thick dark lashes, were as trusting as a child's. "I will try not to be a burden to you."

"You weigh about as much as a bird. You are not a burden."

"I meant I won't be whiny and childish."

"You are hurt, and this isn't going to be a fun-filled sleigh ride, *shpatchen*." The name fitted her. It meant "little sparrow." A tiny creature bold enough to attack a cat that came too close to the nest.

Her lips curved in a soft half smile. "My grandmother used to call me that when I was a child."

It warmed his heart to see her smiling. "Don't worry, Gemma. Everything will be fine."

Despite her throbbing ankle and the biting cold, Gemma relaxed in Jesse's arms. He must not think too badly of her if he could call her by a childish nickname.

She didn't remember the last time she'd felt so safe. Especially around a man.

Until this minute, she had believed any chance of friendship between them had been ruined by her impulsive actions last year. Nothing she could say would undo his opinion except to behave in a manner he expected of a humble Amish maiden. Though he didn't care much for her, she had no doubt he would do his best to protect her and make the journey back to the highway as quickly and safely as possible.

He settled her on his pile of pine branches on the overturned hood. She scooted around until nothing was poking her unbearably and nodded. He took the blanket from her and draped it around her shoulders, pulling it tight beneath her chin. "Ready?"

"I'm ready. Should we leave a note telling Dale where we have gone in case we miss each other?"

"The road is narrow. I don't see how we could miss each other." He walked to the front and slipped his arms through the loops he had made from the tie-downs. He started forward and Gemma grimaced with pain at the jolt. She grabbed at the branches under her with both hands. He looked back.

"I'm fine. I'm fine," she said quickly.

"You don't look fine. What will make it less painful for you? I don't know how long this walk will take, so think about that before you say *fine* again."

He was right. There was no need to suffer more than she had to simply to impress him. "Maybe if I had something higher to sit on and a way to keep my foot propped up a little."

"Will the toolbox be high enough to sit on?"

It was about a foot tall and just as wide. "I think so."

She scooted to one side. He placed the toolbox toward the back of the hood and rearranged the pine insulation on it. Taking the ax, he cut another armful of branches and arranged them as a padded rest for her injured leg. He helped her settle onto them. "How is that?"

"Better. Now all I need is something to hang on to if the terrain gets rougher."

"It will get rougher." He cut another piece of webbing, fashioned it into a big loop and attached it to the front of the hood. He gave her the webbing to hang on to the way she would hold the reins of a horse.

He slipped into his harness and started walking. The seat and padding for her foot made it better but it was a far cry from comfortable. Knowing there was nothing she could do to help Jesse, Gemma gritted her teeth and held on, determined not to complain.

The snow flurries grew heavier. A layer of white soon covered her blanket and the pine needles around her. The wind sent the fresh snow snaking across the trail where breaks in the trees offered access. Jesse's makeshift sled moved easily over the snow, but he couldn't avoid the dips and hollows that jolted her.

They'd gone several miles before her fingers grew numb despite the socks she was using as mittens. She tucked one hand inside her cloak until her fingers stopped stinging, then switched hands to warm the other one. While it helped some, she was soon switching them every few minutes. She tried warming them both at the same time, but the sled hit a drift and she toppled over backward. Jesse was beside her before she managed to right herself.

"Are you okay?"

She sat up and repositioned her aching ankle. "I'm fine."

"What happened?"

"I wasn't hanging on because I was trying to warm my hands inside my cape. I'm sorry."

"Sorry for what? Giving me a break? It's not such a bad idea." He looked around and spotted a place where he could sit on a toppled tree. A group of thick cedars behind it provided a windbreak. He maneuvered the sled up beside them. He knelt at Gemma's side and pulled off his gloves. "Give me your hands."

He peeled off the socks she was using and sandwiched her icy fingers between his warm palms.

Her hands disappeared between his large ones as he gently rubbed the circulation back into them.

Gemma's hands were small and amazingly delicate. They were also ice-cold. His determination to keep her safe grew tenfold. "It shouldn't be much longer. I think we've come at least eight miles. I can't believe we have more than two or three miles left to go."

"I don't see how you can follow the truck's tracks in this snow."

The tire tracks had been obliterated by the blowing snow miles back. "I can't, but I'm sticking to the road." The wider opening between the trees had been his only guide for the past hour.

He realized the socks Gemma had been using for mittens were wet. Putting them back on wouldn't do her any good. He needed a way to keep her upright without having her hang on to anything.

He cut free the webbing she had been holding on to. "What are you doing?" she asked.

"You'll need to keep your hands inside your cloak."

"If your intent is to dump me out in the snow, just say so."

"That's a ridiculous thing to say." He set about making a smaller loop on one end.

"And removing my only way of hanging on isn't silly?"

"You can't put the wet socks back on."

"They will work for a couple more miles," she insisted.

"Nope."

"Fine. Leave me here and go get help."

"Don't be absurd. I'm not leaving you. Raise your arms."

"Why."

"Because I asked you to."

She folded her arms across her chest. "Not until you explain to me what you're doing."

Even cold and miserable, she could be obstinate. He sighed heavily. "I'm making a smaller loop to go around your body. I'm going to fasten the other end of the strap to the front of the hood and pull it tight. That will keep you from falling over backward in the rough places."

"That's all you had to say." She held out her hand. He gave the loop to her. She slipped it over her head and settled it under her arms.

"How is that?" he asked.

She pulled her hands inside her cloak and leaned back several times to test the strength and tension. "It's fine."

"Fine enough to last a few more hours?"

"It's getting dark already."

He held his arms wide. "Want to spend the night here?"

"Of course not. Are you worried that we haven't met up with Dale yet?" Giving voice to her concern made the situation seem even more dire.

"I have enough to worry about getting you to safety." He pulled on his gloves, slipped into his harness and started trudging forward again.

Although Gemma had always been impressed and intimidated by Jesse's size, she had never considered how strong he actually was. Walking through the knee-deep snow and pulling the sled had to be exhausting and yet the only break he had taken was to ensure her comfort. His determination was amazing as he struggled through deeper and deeper snowdrifts. He fell to his knees once but got up and kept going. As darkness fell, Gemma shivered in the increasing cold. The snow finally let up. The clouds overhead thinned out and the thin sickle of the moon cast the landscape in harsh shadows of black on white. She huddled over as low as she could get but the wind still found her and sucked away any warmth from beneath her blanket. When she had reached the end of her endurance, she heard Jesse as he muttered something that sounded like "Finally."

She raised her face to see a break in the trees ahead. She was ready to cheer if her teeth would stop chattering long enough. Her elation died a quick death as Jesse pulled her sled into the open. There wasn't a highway in front of them. Only the remains of some kind of building in a small clearing. A cabin maybe. A chimney jutted above part of the roof that hadn't fallen in. She didn't remember seeing a place like this on their way this morning. Could they have passed by and she just hadn't noticed the building? She listened but didn't hear the sounds of traffic. Nor did she see any lights.

Jesse dropped to his knees and bowed his head. Fear sent a surge of adrenaline through her aching body. "Jesse, are you okay? Where are we?"

He looked back at her, but his face was in the shadows and she couldn't read his expression. "We're lost."

Chapter Five

Jesse couldn't believe what lay in front of him. Not safety but desolation. The ruins of a second building were nothing more than odd blackened timbers sticking upright through the snow. A pond sat frozen and silent at the bottom of the clearing. A dead cedar tree stood between the house and the pond. There were no signs of life anywhere. He didn't bother calling out.

Somehow, he had made a horrible mistake. He had no idea where he had taken a wrong turn. It was his fault and his alone. He'd been in such a hurry to get back to New Covenant that he'd left his good sense behind. They should have stayed with the truck. They might have been rescued by now.

He wouldn't be at the auction in the morning. The land he'd hoped to buy would go to someone else. Now he was lost in the wilderness and, worst of all, he'd brought Gemma with him into this dangerous situation. He sank to his heels as the magnitude of what he had done overwhelmed him and bowed his head.

Please, Lord, give me the strength to overcome this disaster. Help me keep Gemma safe.

He repeated the phrase over and over in his mind, searching for the solace he needed. "Jesse, you have to get up."

It wasn't the voice of his heavenly Father, but rather the voice of the little sparrow on the sled. If she had once thought him as dense as a post, he had certainly proved her right. His bold assertion that he could get them back to the highway was nothing but an empty promise.

He looked at her over his shoulder. Would she forgive him for putting her life in danger? "I'm sorry, Gemma. I don't know where I went wrong."

"That doesn't matter, Jesse. We need shelter. We need a fire." She could barely talk because her teeth were chattering so badly.

She was right. Now wasn't the time for remorse and self-pity. He struggled to his feet and pulled the sled toward the cabin. The snow had drifted as high as the front porch. The structure blocked the wind from the north. He stepped onto the floorboards carefully. They seemed solid enough. He slipped out of his harness and pulled open the front door. It scraped along the floor but opened wide enough for him to get inside.

It was too dark to see much. The smell of charred wood filled his nostrils, but the ceiling seemed intact and the interior was free of snow. As his eyes adjusted to the gloom, he saw a stone fireplace dominated the center of the space. It was a double-sided type open to two separate rooms. The cabin would provide the shelter they needed if he could get a fire going.

He went back outside and lifted Gemma from her sled. She was shivering violently. He carried her inside and lowered her to the floor. "I'll get a fire started."

"You have m-matches?" she managed to ask through chattering teeth.

"*Nee*, but there is a small propane torch with a lighter in Dale's toolbox. I'm right glad we brought it along."

"Me—me too."

He carried in the tool chest and found the propane canister. "Please don't let it be empty," he muttered. He turned the valve on and clicked it once. The bright orange-and-blue flame pushed back the shadows. The room was empty except for some tattered lace curtains on the windows and a small stack of logs beside the fireplace. Using the torch and one of the curtains as tinder, he quickly got a fire going. The flicker of the orange flames catching hold was the most beautiful thing he had seen in his life.

"Thank You, Lord." Gemma pulled herself closer to the blaze. She was still shivering. Jesse helped her sit up and positioned himself next to her. He took off her wet bonnet. The blanket was too damp to be useful, but thankfully, her cloak was dry.

He unbuttoned his coat. "Lean against me."

She was too weak or too cold to object. "You should take off your cloak."

"I'd rather keep it on."

"Okay." The warmth of his body kept the cold of the room away from her. He rubbed his hands up and down her arms to get the blood flowing.

"*Danki*," she muttered.

He didn't know how long they sat together, letting the warmth of the fire drive the chill away. Eventually her shivering stopped. Her head dropped back against his chest. From her even breathing, he knew she had fallen asleep. He needed to get more wood. He should also take stock of the rest of the house, but for some reason he was reluctant to move. It was more than the simple fact that he didn't want to wake her. It just felt right to have his arms around her. To have her head resting against him with such trust. It was a foolish thought. He already knew what she thought of him. *Big as an ox and dumb as a post.*

He didn't want to wake her. When she recouped her energy, she would realize the full extent of his blunder. He'd taken them out of the frying pan and into the fire, only it was more like out of the refrigerator and into the freezer. He shifted his position slightly on the wood floor. Her breathing changed. He stiffened. Was she awake? He couldn't see her face.

It took Gemma a few seconds to realize where she was. A warm fire crackled in front of her in an unfamiliar fireplace made of rough rocks. She knew Jesse sat beside her with a hand on her shoulder. Her head rested against his chest. The soles of her feet were too warm, so she pulled them to the side. He stopped breathing when she drew up her feet. She remained still, hoping he would, as well. If he knew she was awake, he would move away in a heartbeat. Just for a little while, she wanted to give thanks that they were both alive and pretend he was holding her because he wanted to and not because he was trying to keep her warm.

His breathing resumed. She smiled to herself and closed her eyes. It seemed she was to be granted a few more minutes to enjoy the comfort and security of his embrace. A moment later, a tiny flutter in her abdomen reminded her why she was in this situation at all.

The baby was kicking, proving he or she was okay

despite the difficult ride and grueling temperature Gemma had endured. She hadn't been able to think of her mistake as her baby until recently. It was something she hadn't allowed herself to dwell on before now. The flutter came again. She didn't want to think about the baby or the baby's father. She sat bolt upright. Jesse withdrew his arm as she knew he would.

There wasn't any comfort meant for her. There were only problems to be solved.

"I'm warm enough now," she said. "Do you know where we are?"

He scooted away and stood up. "As I said before, we're lost."

He tossed a log on the fire and lit Dale's propane torch. "I want to check out the rest of the cabin to see if there is anything we can use."

She looked around at the bare floor and walls and tried for a touch of humor. "A cedar chest full of quilts would be nice. However, from the condition of this room, I would say I'm being overly optimistic."

"*Ja.*"

His dry comeback proved her attempt at being funny had missed the mark. Without Jesse next to her, a cold draft began seeping through her clothing. Jesse stared at her for a moment, then went outside. He reappeared a few minutes later, pulling the truck hood sideways through the door and carrying the toolbox.

It was on the tip of her tongue to ask what he was doing, but she decided this time she would just wait and see.

He propped the makeshift sled up against the wall. He went out and returned this time with all the pine branches that had served as a cushion for her. He still didn't offer an explanation, although he did glance at her. She smiled brightly, knowing her cheerfulness and lack of questions would surprise him. He thought of her as a nuisance. If he had it in mind that she was going to be difficult, she would show him she had matured in her time away. His brows drew together as he studied her face. It was the expression she was used to seeing whenever she was in his company.

Still, without comment, he pushed open the door that led to another part of the cabin. From the light he carried, she could see him shove aside a layer of snow. He disappeared into the room. She waited for him to report back. Exhaustion pulled at her eyelids and she closed them. She opened them quickly when she started to tip over. "I am so tired I can fall asleep sitting up," she muttered.

Why was she still sitting up? She wadded her bonnet into a pathetic pillow and lay down on her side close to the fire. Something hard poked her. She withdrew the forgotten water bottles from the pocket of her cloak, sat up and drank one. She set the other bottle where Jesse could see it and lay down again.

Sometime later, Jesse woke her by shaking her shoulder. "Gemma, the floor is too cold for you to sleep on."

She lifted her head. "Don't tell me you found a bed."

"*Nee*, but I have made one."

There was an inviting pile of fragrant, soft pine boughs covered with the blanket made up beside her. "How nice. You are a rather handy man, Jesse Crump."

"I try."

He helped her stand. She sucked in a quick breath at the pain in her ankle. "Sorry," he said.

"It's going to hurt no matter what I do."

"Would you like me to make another cold pack for it?"

She repressed a shiver. *"Nee."*

She hobbled to the bed, lay down and wriggled into a slightly more comfortable position so that she could see him. "Where are you going to sleep?"

He pointed at the fireplace. "In the room on the other side. I can see you and hear you if you need anything."

Sometime while she slept, he had made a brace to hold the truck hood on its side a foot or so past the head of her bedding. It reflected the heat from the fire back toward her and cut the uncomfortable draft she had noticed before. "Did you find anything useful in the other rooms?"

"I found a cast-iron skillet with a broken handle in what was left of the kitchen."

"Did you find some eggs and bacon to go with it?"

He scowled at her. "What do you think?"

"I'm trying to make light of the situation, Jesse. Never mind. Anything else?"

"Nothing useful. I'll take a closer look in the daylight. It appears a fire destroyed the back half of the building. Only these two rooms are intact."

"For which I give grateful thanks to the Lord. What time is it?"

"Around ten o'clock."

"What do you think happened to Dale?"

"I wish I knew. Do you need anything before I go?"

She shook her head and immediately prayed for Dale's safety, upset that she'd barely given him a thought throughout the afternoon and evening.

Jesse crossed through the archway to the other side of the fireplace. She waited until he had settled himself on his bedding. The outline of his body shimmered in the flames. "Is it possible no one is looking for us?"

"It's possible if something happened to Dale and he didn't reach the highway." Jesse turned onto his side, facing away from her.

The moment the idea occurred to her, it wouldn't go away. What if Dale was lost himself? Or worse. She and Jesse could be stranded for only God knew how long. Was it still snowing? "Will they be able to follow our tracks to this place if someone is looking for us?"

"I don't know that either."

"What do you know?" she snapped.

"I know I'm dead tired and I don't want to answer any more questions about things beyond my control. Go to sleep, Gemma."

"That's easy for you to say," she muttered.

She sat up and wrapped her arms tightly across her chest. They were stranded in some out-of-the-way place and it was possible no one knew they were lost. She touched her head to make sure her prayer *kapp* was still on.

Please, Lord, help us. I know I haven't spoken to You much lately. I've been too ashamed. I'm trusting in Your mercy now for Jesse and Dale. And for my baby's sake, for this child, who is the most innocent among us.

Her panic subsided. She was in His hands. He would care for Jesse and her and the child she carried. She had to believe God would see them through this.

She glanced around the room. Sometime while she slept, Jesse had replenished the wood beside the fire. The bright color on the inside proved the logs were newly split. He hadn't found a cut pile ready to use. He had split it with a small hatchet out in the bitter cold.

He had expended a lot of energy to make sure they could stay warm.

"Jesse," she said softly.

"What?" Exasperation filled that one word to the limit.

He almost convinced her to remain silent but she couldn't. "I think you saved my life today. I appreciate all you have done for me. *Danki.*"

He gave a deep sigh. "You're welcome. Do me one favor in return?"

"Stop talking?"

"Ja."

This time his succinct answer didn't annoy her. It was just Jesse's way. She lay down and closed her eyes. The morning would bring light to see by. They would retrace their steps and find the logging road. After that, they would reach safety in a few hours. She would be back in New Covenant by nightfall.

Where her real troubles would make today seem like nothing more than a winter outing.

Jesse woke to a cold draft blowing over him and the sound of Gemma being sick. He rolled off his bedding and got to his feet. Every muscle in his body ached in protest but that didn't matter. Something was wrong with Gemma.

He came around the fireplace. She had somehow made it out the front door and was leaning over the porch railing. He stood two feet away, unsure of what to do. "What's wrong, Gemma?"

She straightened up. Her face was pale. She managed a slight smile as she dabbed at the corner of her mouth with one of her handkerchiefs. "We can rule out that it was something I ate."

How could she be making a joke at a time like this? "Are you okay?"

"As okay as I can be in the situation. Can you help me back inside?" She held out one hand.

"Of course." He swept her up into his arms.

She squeaked in protest but then she laid her head against his shoulder when he ignored her. "I meant for you to hold my arm while I hobble back inside."

"This is quicker." He kicked the door all the way open and carried her to her bedding. After laying her down, he went back to close the door. He returned to her side and thrust his hands into his coat pockets. "What do you need?"

She sat up and drew her knees up under her cloak. "Nothing. I'm fine."

"You use that word far too often. How can you be fine if you just threw up?"

"You have a point. I would love a cup of hot tea and a cracker. Any chance that Dale left some in his toolbox?"

"I'll check. Chamomile or Earl Grey?"

Her eyes widened with surprise. "Jesse Crumb made a joke. He has a sense of humor."

"Don't look so amazed." He stoked the fire, added another log and sat cross-legged on the floor. The auction would be taking place soon. He wondered who would get the land he'd had his heart set on.

"I noticed it was snowing again while I was on the porch. Heavily. No one will be able to follow our tracks, will they…?" Her voice trailed away.

"Nope." At least she understood why help wouldn't be coming.

"So, what do we do?"

"The hardest thing of all in a survival situation. Stay put."

Her eyes grew wide. "When you say survival situation, are you telling me that we are in serious trouble?"

There was a long silence. "*Ja.* We are."

She pressed a hand to her forehead. "I know conversation is hard for you, Jesse, but please spell it out for me and don't sugarcoat it. How much trouble are we in?"

"On the downside, we are lost and away from our vehicle, where they will be looking for us as soon as the weather clears. That is, if Dale made it out. If he didn't, then no one will be looking for us until we don't return to New Covenant. The bishop won't expect us to travel in bad weather. He may assume we have hunkered down to wait it out. In that case, it may be a week or more before someone starts searching. Are they likely to be looking along a remote logging road? I doubt it, unless someone noticed us turning onto it when we left the highway."

"You could've left a little sugar on it. That was the downside. Now, what is the upside?"

"We have a roof over our heads and a way to stay warm."

"That's it?"

"Pretty much."

She clasped her fingers together. "I see."

She wasn't hysterical or crying. Jesse gave thanks for that. She sat quietly, staring into the fire for a few minutes. When she finally looked at him, her eyes were filled with determination.

"I'm going to need a crutch, so I can move around and you don't have to carry me everywhere."

It was a reasonable request. "I can do that."

"Water is important. I drank the last of mine. Did you find yours?"

He nodded once. "I did. I drank it last night too. There's plenty of snow to melt so we won't go thirsty."

"I also noticed some rose bushes growing beside the house while I was outside. If you can gather some rose hips for me, I'll make some tea. Where is the skillet you found?"

"Still in the kitchen. I'll fetch it after I make you a crutch. How is the ankle?"

"Black-and-blue from what I can see of it around the edge of the tape. I didn't take your handiwork off. It hurts when I move, but it will be fine as long as I'm careful."

"How is your stomach?"

She blushed, although he wasn't sure why. "It will be fine." She paused and looked at him. "I mean, it is *goot* now."

He tried to reassure her. "Hope for the best and prepare for the worst. I will take care of you, Gemma."

"I know that. See if you can find anything usable in the other part of the house and bring me that pan packed with snow. I'll need hot water if I'm going to make tea."

Her attitude amazed him. Perhaps he had underestimated her in the past. Or perhaps the worst was yet to come. He was never quite certain where Gemma was concerned.

Chapter Six

Gemma discovered the skillet was a small shallow one, only six inches across, but usable after Jesse chopped a hole through the ice on the pond and scrubbed it clean. He brought in a large handful of rose hips for her on his way back. She removed the seeds and placed the pulp in the skillet filled with melting snow to simmer. Soon the delightful aroma made her stomach rumble. Jesse disappeared outside again.

It was still snowing heavily. She could hear the sound of the wind increasing. It would soon turn into a full-blown blizzard if the storm kept building. The creaking of the old cabin worried her as much as the weather. Was it strong enough to support the snow that was falling? Would it collapse and bury them alive? It had clearly survived a few winters. But would it last through one more? Where would they find shelter if it came down?

To Gemma's delight, Jesse returned a short time later with a long thick branch he had whittled into a crutch. She happily tried it out. It was good to be upright without hopping on one foot, but the crutch was too tall. "Can you shorten it?"

"How much shorter does it need to be?"

"Take off an inch. That should be enough."

He started to whittle at the end. "If I cut off any more I will have to give it to a crippled mouse to use."

"Are you making fun of my size?" She held up one hand. "Wait. Don't answer that. First, I have to apologize for comments I made to you in the past. If I hurt your feelings, I'm truly sorry, Jesse. I wasn't always kind."

"Like when you said I was as big as an ox and dumb as a post? You weren't far wrong, but I forgive you."

"*Danki.* That means a lot. And I was wrong. You may be a big man, but you aren't dumb and it was cruel of me to say that. Now, what were you saying about mice?"

"Nothing." He handed back the shortened crutch. "See if this works better."

She took it and made a trip across the room and back. "This is *goot*." She wished there was some way to pad the part under her arm. She was still wearing three layers of clothing and her cloak. She didn't want to sacrifice warmth for a little comfort nor did she want Jesse to give her the shirt off his back, which she knew he was more than capable of doing. "Did you happen to find anything we could use as cups?"

He shook his head. "All I found was a broken pint jar. The edge is too jagged to drink out of, but we can melt snow in it. I found a few broken plates, nothing else we can use."

"If you can cut the necks off our water bottles we can use those as glasses."

"That is easy enough."

She lowered herself to the floor in front of the fire. After Jesse was finished with the water bottles, he sat beside her. Gemma folded her apron to use as a hot pad. She moved the skillet away from the fire and after letting it cool a bit she poured the rose hip tea into the plastic bottles and handed one to Jesse. He took a sip and wrinkled his nose.

She smothered a smile. "Did you know rose hips have more vitamin C than oranges? Do you like it?"

"I've had worse. It's not coffee, but it's warm."

Gemma took a sip of hers. "It's better with honey, but it is hot and that makes it taste *wunderbar* to me."

"I'm not surprised. You haven't had anything to eat since supper the night before last."

She grimaced. "I couldn't eat that greasy hamburger. I threw it out."

"When was the last time you ate? Tell me the truth."

"The morning before I arrived in Cleary I had a good breakfast."

"And you let me eat your burrito yesterday morning? What were you thinking?"

"That I didn't want to eat a spicy breakfast and bump about in Dale's truck for hours afterward. My stomach doesn't travel well. I get carsick."

"You weren't in a car this morning."

She didn't want to tell him she had morning sickness, so she skirted around the issue. "Perhaps not, but I was exhausted after a terrible day and uncomfortable night. I'm fine now. I'm even hungry. I could eat a moose if you want to go out and wrestle one to the ground."

He stared at her for several long seconds. "I'm sorry I got us lost."

"It was a mistake anyone could have made. You

might remember I was with you. The conditions were horrible. I'm amazed you had the strength to get us this far."

"I thought you would be angry."

"I'm too tired to pitch a fit. Tomorrow I'll harp at you." She took another sip of tea. He made her uncomfortable with his intense scrutiny. A few months ago, she might have been upset with him over getting them lost and taken her frustration out on him. Everything changed the day she found out that the baby's father had left town without a word. She'd had to grow up in a hurry.

What would Jesse think of her when he found out? New Covenant was a tiny settlement. Everyone would know within a matter of days, unless her parents agreed to keep her secret. She couldn't hide it for long unless she left the community. She was already six months along. Perhaps her parents would allow her to stay with her aunt or one of her cousins in rural Pennsylvania. She could have the baby and give it up for adoption. After that, she could return to New Covenant with no one the wiser, except a few close family members. Only, would she be able to give up her baby?

It was the first time she realized that she actually thought of the child as *her baby*. She pressed a hand to her heart.

"What are you thinking?" he asked.

Startled by his question, she shook her head. "Nothing. Why?"

"You looked sad. Are you worried about being stuck here?"

She splayed her fingers over her abdomen under her cloak. There was more than her own life at stake if rescue didn't come soon. "Shouldn't I be worried? You're the one who took the sugar off my expectations when you laid out our situation."

"Maybe I made it sound too bleak."

"*Nee*, I would rather know the truth."

"Food will be our most pressing need soon, although we can survive without it for several weeks."

"What is your plan?"

He cocked his head to the side. "What makes you think I have a plan?"

"Well, you aren't screaming hysterically and running in circles shouting, 'We're going to die!' You managed impressively by improvising a sled to move me, collected firewood and even figured out how to use the truck hood as a draft blocker. One might think you do this kind of thing every winter."

"I get in a lot of hunting by myself, and survival skills are important."

Most of the Amish men she knew hunted for food. A deer or moose was a welcome addition to a family's freezer. "Did Dale leave a rifle in his toolbox?" she asked hopefully.

Jesse actually smiled. He had a sweet smile and a dimple in his left cheek she had never noticed before. "I wish he had."

"What kind of hunting can you do with a wrench set and a screwdriver?"

"Not much, but I can fashion small game snares from my bootlaces. There is always the pond at the bottom of the clearing. It might be possible to catch fish through the ice. It isn't thick enough yet to walk on it. There are cattails I can harvest. The inner bark of the white pine tree is edible, and we have plenty of those around us.

You can also make tea from the pine needles. They're high in vitamin C too. We won't starve if I can help it."

Jesse became more animated as he talked about how to harvest the edible parts of trees, something Gemma never thought she would consider as a part of her diet. She would have to eat something for the sake of the babe. She asked a few more questions to keep him talking. She'd never seen him like this. Where had this Jesse been hiding? Maybe he had just been waiting for someone to listen.

She'd first found him attractive because he was a strong, work-driven man. And to be honest, he'd been one of only two single Amish fellows in the area. Now that she had a glimpse of the man underneath the brawn, she liked him even more.

"How did you learn all of this stuff?"

He suddenly seemed to realize he had been talking too much. "Here and there."

"Come on. Where?"

He looked away and tossed a twig into the fire. "When I first came to Maine, I took some survival training courses the local game warden taught."

"When I first came to Maine I invested in a very heavy coat, fur-lined boots and a lot of books to read. Why are you embarrassed to say you took classes?"

"Because most people don't think a big man like me is very bright."

Shame brought a lump to her throat. He said most people, but he was actually saying Gemma Lapp. "You really like it here, don't you?"

"I love owning my own farm. It's small, but it's mine. I had plans to expand, but that has gone by the wayside."

"Why?"

"Some land next to mine unexpectedly came up for auction. I was determined to purchase it but missed my chance."

"Because someone outbid you?"

"*Nee*, the auction took place this morning."

"If you hadn't stayed with me at the truck, you could have made it back to the highway and gotten home in time."

He shrugged. "There's no way to know that for sure. Why do you hate this country so much?"

She moved a little farther from the fire and stretched out her feet, wincing as she moved her bad ankle. "*Hate* is a strong word. I wasn't prepared for how lonely it could be. I was used to lots of friends and cousins visiting back and forth in our community in Pennsylvania. In New Covenant, I had only two friends. My cousin Anna and Bethany Martin. They both married last year, and they naturally had less time for a single friend."

"And you thought marriage would be the answer for you too?"

Jesse watched as Gemma's cheeks flushed a deep pink. She folded her hands together and stared at them. "I wondered when that would come up."

"It was a joke to you, wasn't it?" He braced himself to hear her answer. "Little woman tames the big ox and breaks him to harness."

Her gaze flew to his face. "*Nee*, it was never a joke."

"Wasn't it?"

"I can see why you thought so. I acted foolishly, but I did like you, Jesse. I do like you. I'm sorry if you thought I was trying to make fun of you or to hurt you. That wasn't my reason."

"So what prompted your pursuit of me?"

"I guess I wanted what my friends had found. They were both so content. You were the best choice out of the single men in New Covenant at the time."

He snorted, unwilling to accept her explanation. "You expect me to believe you chose me over handsome, well-to-do Jedidiah Zook? I'm not stupid."

"I never thought you were, but you can be very stubborn. I reckon I saw it as a challenge. Besides, Jedidiah Zook is no prize. He thinks more of himself than any woman he knows."

Was she telling the truth? Jesse tried to recall the things she had said and done before her stunning proposal of marriage. She'd never shown an interest in Jedidiah that he could recall. Had he misjudged her and her motives all this time? He could believe that she saw winning him as a challenge. That made sense. It was more believable than thinking she had suddenly fallen in love with him. Her confession that she liked him soothed some of his past hurts. He liked her too but couldn't bring himself to say so.

He leaned back on his elbows. "It's all in the past and best forgotten." It was a relief to be able to say the words and mean it.

"Agreed. I was a foolish girl used to getting my own way."

"So what changed you?"

She stared at her hands again. He noticed her fingers were clenched tightly together as her expression grew sad. "We all get wiser as we get older."

There was more to that story, but he didn't want to press her. Something had to have happened in Florida that had changed the brash girl he knew into the somber woman sitting with him now. Maybe one day she would feel comfortable enough to share that sorrow with him.

And why was he thinking about continuing to see Gemma?

When they got out of this mess, he was certain she wouldn't want to spend another hour in his company. "Why don't you take a nap if you're tired? We don't have anything else to do."

"That's a fine idea." She sighed heavily and lay down, turning on her side with her back to him. Her tea sat unfinished on the floor beside her. Was she sicker than she was letting on? There was nothing he could do for her if that were the case. He wasn't used to the feeling of total helplessness.

Jesse was able to venture outside when the wind died down in the early afternoon. He took the opportunity to strip two of the closest pine trees of their bark as high as he could reach. He regretted that his actions would ultimately kill the trees, so he limited his harvest to what they could use in the next day or two. At the pond, he found cattails growing in the shallow end. Pulling up the roots and washing them was an ice-cold messy business. By the time he got back to the cabin, both of his wet hands were numb.

Gemma immediately noticed he didn't have his gloves on. She knocked the cattail rhizomes to the floor and began to dry his hands with her apron. "Are you trying to get frostbite?"

"I was trying to get our supper."

"I would go hungry another night rather than see you wet up to your elbows in this frigid temperature. Do you have any feeling in them?"

"Not at the moment. I'll be okay."

"Come over to the window." She pulled him to the grimy glass where the light was better. She turned his hands over and inspected them carefully.

"Satisfied?" he asked, pleased that she was making a fuss over him.

"You have some blanched skin and some small blisters. I've seen worse frostbite. Go warm them by the fire, but be careful until all the feeling comes back. I don't want you going out any more today. You're trying to do too much. I could go to bed happy if all I had to eat was a few more stewed rose hips."

"Speak for yourself. I like meat and potatoes for my supper."

Her scowl disappeared, and she started laughing. He cocked his head slightly. "What's so funny?"

"You like meat and potatoes but you bring home tree bark and roots. I hope you know how to cook this stuff because I certainly don't. Go warm up. What am I supposed to do with these dirty things?" She stared at the stringy rhizomes on the floor.

"Peel them like a potato. You can use my knife."

Jesse sat cross-legged by the fire with his hands, palms up, on his knees. The dull numb sensation was giving way to painful pins and needles. He took his mind off the discomfort by watching Gemma deal with their unusual food. With instructions from him, she prepared their evening meal. Small strips of the pine bark were roasted on a flat stone in front of the fire along with the cattail roots. She served up the fare on two of the broken plates he had found. She sat down on her bedding with a sigh.

"How is your ankle?"

She held her foot out and wiggled her toes. "The

swelling has gone down some. I should be able to get my shoe back on."

"Stay off of it for a while yet and use the crutch."

She munched a piece of roasted pine bark. "This stuff isn't bad. Kind of sweet and crunchy. It doesn't taste like wood, really. Still, I don't think it will ever make the menu at a fast-food restaurant."

"It's okay for now, but I'll try for some meat tomorrow if the weather is clear. I've seen plenty of rabbit tracks in the snow. I'll set out some snares tomorrow morning and check them tomorrow evening."

"If the weather is clear, don't you think we should try to get back to the highway or the truck?"

"I'm tempted to say yes, but the truth is I have no idea which way to go. I thought I was following the road we came in on, but I could have taken a wrong turn one mile after we left the truck or five miles after we left it. *Gott* was *goot* in leading us to this shelter. We are safest staying put. I will make a distress sign in the clearing that can be seen from the air in case someone is looking for us. The problem is, every time it snows, it will be covered up."

"The next time we end up in a situation like this, I'm going to ask for the sugarcoated version." She pushed her food away.

"Let us pray there won't ever be a next time."

"Amen," she said emphatically.

The next morning, Jesse woke to the sound of Gemma's crutch tapping the floor as she hurried across the room and out the door. A few seconds later, he heard her retching. She was sick again. Concern pushed away his reluctance to confront her about it. He waited until she came through the door and returned to her bedding.

"It's not car sickness. What's wrong with you? And don't tell me you are fine."

"It's not something for you to worry about, Jesse."

Too late. He was already worried. "But you're not going to tell me what's wrong."

"I'm going to be blunt. It's none of your business."

"As long as we are stranded together, I think it is."

Sighing heavily, she lay down and turned away from him. "I'm going back to sleep now."

She had barely eaten anything last night. How sick was she? Maybe what she needed was real food, a hearty broth or rabbit stew. She couldn't stand to lose much weight. She was tiny enough as it was. He took his responsibility to care for her seriously.

He sat up and began to pull the laces out of his work boots. The sooner he got snares set, the sooner he could bring back fresh meat for her. When he had what he needed, he cut one lace in half, using it to secure his boots while he used the rest to fashion another snare.

He quietly left the cabin. Outside, he found it had stopped snowing during the night. He took his hatchet and cut several armloads of pine branches. He arranged them into a large X about ten feet long in the center of the clearing. Satisfied with the result, he took his snares and walked into the woods.

The sound of an airplane in the distance sent him racing back into the open. Were they searching for Gemma and him? He looked up but couldn't see it.

Gemma came out onto the porch. "Do I hear a plane?"

"*Ja*, but where is it?" The sound told him it was moving closer but the tall trees around them blocked his view.

"I can't see it."

They kept looking but Jesse realized the sound was now moving away from them.

"Where are they going?" He heard the panic in her voice.

"They may be flying a search pattern. If they are, they will come back. We have to pray they fly over our clearing and see the distress sign."

"If we make a signal fire, the smoke will rise above the trees. Shall I add more wood to the fire inside?"

"We need something quicker and bigger." How much time did they have? He could still hear the drone of the engine.

"Jesse, what about that dead cedar?"

He looked around and his gaze fell on the brown cedar tree between the cabin and the pond. It was only about eight feet tall, but it would go up in flames easily and produce more smoke faster than building up the fire inside. "Get me the propane torch."

He raced to the porch. Gemma came out and tossed the canister to him. He rushed to the cedar, turned on the torch and clicked the striker. It caught immediately. He shook the snow from the tree and held the torch to it. The tinder-dry branches caught fire and smoke billowed into the air. He stepped back. The flames quickly engulfed the tree, sending orange flames leaping high in the air.

Gemma hobbled toward him through the knee-deep snow. She stumbled, and he caught her before she fell. She clung to his arm as she searched the sky. "Do you think they saw it?"

Chapter Seven

Gemma clutched Jesse's arm as she strained to hear the plane returning. She prayed fervently for their rescue. "Surely they must see the smoke."

He covered Gemma's hands with his own. "Wait, I think I hear it again."

She caught the sound then too. "Please, dear Lord, let them see us."

Suddenly a small aircraft burst into view, barely skimming the tops of the trees. Gemma and Jesse began to shout and wave their arms. The plane circled back once, and it dipped its wing to acknowledge them.

"They saw us!" Gemma threw her arms around Jesse's neck. His bear hug lifted her feet off the ground. She captured his face between her hands. "We're going to be rescued."

As she stared into his eyes, something changed. His pupils darkened as he gazed at her.

"I'm almost sorry we can't stay a little longer," he said softly.

"Why?" The word sounded breathless as it dissipated in the cold air.

"Because I was just beginning to get to know you."

His revelation gave way to a warm comforting sensation followed by sharp loss. She was in his arms. Exactly where she had wanted to be so long ago, and he was still completely out of her reach. Now more than ever. She didn't deserve this man's affection.

Tears pricked the back of her eyes. She moved her hands to his shoulders and he slowly lowered her to the ground. He didn't release her. She couldn't look into his eyes. "And I have learned a lot about you. You enjoy eating bark. Who would've guessed that?"

"And you like to keep secrets," he said, tipping his head to see her face better.

"At least we don't have to do a lot of packing," she said, trying to change the subject.

He seemed to take the hint. "It may be a while before they can get snowmobiles to us. I should get you back inside."

She looked around for her crutch, but he simply swept her up in his arms and walked slowly toward the cabin. She relaxed in his arms. It would be the last time he held her. She wanted the moment to last forever. He stopped at the porch steps. "We've had quite an adventure, haven't we?"

"We did. I imagine you'll be glad to be rid of me." She bit the corner of her lip as she waited for his answer.

"I think I'm going to miss your scolding but not your rose hip tea."

"I wasn't that hard to get along with, was I?"

"Not at all. Well, not most of the time." He smiled slightly. She caught sight of his dimple again. Perhaps she would see it more often now that they had gotten to know each other better.

"At least we won't have to eat bark for supper again tonight."

He chuckled as he gazed into her eyes. "I can always bring some to your house. You should try it fried in a little oil. It's a lot better that way. I think your *daed* might like it."

She looked down. If only she could enjoy his company at home with her parents. She wasn't sure how they would react to her news. She could be shunned. Until she figured out what she was going to do, she couldn't make any plans. "I'm getting cold. You had better take me inside."

"Oh, sure. The last thing you need is frostbitten toes on top of your other problem."

Her gaze snapped to his. Had he put two and two together and come up with her pregnancy as the cause of her illness each morning. "What do you mean?"

"Your sprained ankle. What did you think I meant?" He walked up the steps and carried her through the door, and then he placed her gently on her bedding in front of the fire.

"It doesn't matter. Can you help me get my shoe on?"

"Sure." He knelt and tenderly slipped her walking shoe over her foot. He pulled the laces snug and tied a neat bow. "How does that feel?"

"Good enough to get home. I'm anxious to know what happened to Dale."

He straightened, took a step back and thrust his hands in the pockets of his coat. "Me too. I sure hope he's okay."

"He must be, or they wouldn't have known to look for us." She glanced at their collection of broken pottery, plastic bottles and the sad skillet missing its handle. "I think I'm going to miss this place."

"I'm ready for my own mattress and quilts."

She smothered a smile. "I'm ready for my mother's home cooking."

It was several hours before their rescuers arrived. Two men on snowmobiles as Jesse had predicted. One snowmobile pulled a sled behind it. Jesse went out to speak with the men. After a few minutes, he brought them in to meet her. "These fellows are members of the Wilderness Search and Rescue Team. Bradley is a paramedic. He needs to check us out before they can transport us."

Jesse and the other rescuer stepped back outside to wait. From Bradley's pointed questions, Gemma knew Jesse had told him about her brief bouts of sickness. Satisfied with her blood pressure and pulse, he examined her foot. "Someone did a nice job of stabilizing it with duct tape."

"Jesse thought of it."

The paramedic cut off her stocking and the gray tape. After gentle probing, he looked her straight in the eye. "This will need an X-ray. You may have a broken bone."

"I'll see a doctor when I get home."

"We will take you straight to the hospital from here. Did Jesse have any injuries that you know of?"

"You should check his hands. They were red with white patches of frostbite yesterday."

The paramedic put his equipment away. "I will have the sled ready in a few minutes. We'll have you both checked out at the hospital. It's protocol."

Jesse came in a few minutes later with a large orange blanket. "This should keep you warm on the ride." He draped it around her and scooped her up again. He carried her out to the snowmobile. She was going to miss this easy familiarity. She knew he would behave very differently once they were back in New Covenant. "Did you ask about Dale?"

"I did. He hit his head much harder than we thought. He made it down to the highway, but he passed out at the side of the road. Someone found him and got him to the hospital. He didn't wake up until the next day. The weather was too bad to look for us then."

Their second rescuer was a teenage boy. "Mr. Kaufman gave us directions to his truck. When we discovered it was empty, we started an air and ground search for the two of you."

"We are certainly grateful for your help," Jesse said as he settled her onto the sled and tucked the blanket around her.

Gemma bit her lip. Had he noticed her rounded tummy? If he had, his expression hadn't changed. The men then covered her with another blanket and strapped her in. It was an odd sensation to be lying flat while the men prepared to get underway. It was even more so once they were moving.

Her view consisted of the blue sky overhead and the tops of the tall pines that bordered the trail. It wasn't long before the speed of the trees zipping past made her queasy. She closed her eyes for the remainder of the trip. When they finally stopped, she opened them to see more men in uniforms waiting for them beside an ambulance.

She was transferred from the sled to a gurney in the ambulance. Jesse was allowed to ride beside her. She was grateful for his solid, calm presence.

Once they reached the hospital, they were taken

to separate rooms in the emergency department. The nurse who took her vital signs and asked all manner of questions was extremely kind and curious about her adventure. She gave Gemma a gown to change into and stepped out of the room. Gemma was waiting to be seen by a doctor when Jesse spoke on the other side of the curtain. "May I come in?"

Although the hospital gown she wore was perfectly modest, she drew the sheet up to her chin and turned on her side to hide her growing waistline. "Come in, Jesse."

The concern in his eyes warmed her heart. "How are you? And don't say fine."

"I am wonderfully warm, but this bed isn't the most comfortable. How are you?"

He held out his left hand. He had a bandage wrapped around it. "They say I am in perfect health, except for some small patches of skin on my hand that may slough off. They gave me some cream to use."

"I'm sorry to hear that. The cattail roots were not worth it."

He grinned. "I thought they were pretty good. You just weren't hungry enough to appreciate them. Maybe a little bird like you could live on rose hips, but a man my size needed something more substantial. As soon as they let us out of here, we are going to get some burgers and fries."

"That sounds *wunderbar.*"

A young man wearing a white coat with a stethoscope around his neck stepped into the room. He held a clipboard in his hand. The nurse who had questioned Gemma earlier came in and stood behind him. He read silently for a minute or two and then looked up with a smile. "Miss Lapp? I'm Dr. Johnson. It sounds like you have had a tough time of it lately."

Jesse tipped his head toward the door. "I'll be out in the waiting room. I want to call the bishop and explain what happened to us. I'm sure he is concerned."

The nurse nodded. "I'll come get you when we're finished. You might want to go by the registration desk. They have questions about insurance."

Jesse stopped at the doorway. "We Amish don't carry insurance. Our church will cover what is owed if it is more than we can pay. I'll take care of your bill, Gemma."

"*Danki*, Jesse. My father will repay you."

"I know. I'm not worried about that."

Once Jesse was out of the room, Gemma took a deep breath. "There is something you should know doctor. I'm pregnant."

"Congratulations. We'll make sure to shield your baby while we x-ray your foot."

She managed to thank him. He had no way of knowing this wasn't a happy event for her, and she didn't share that part of her history. He gave her a thorough examination. His friendly smile changed to a look of concern as he listened for the baby's heartbeat.

Gemma started to worry. "Is everything okay?"

"Your little one seems to be hiding from me. Have you noticed any changes? Has there been a decrease in movement?"

"*Nee.*" Her hands clenched the sheet tightly.

"Let's make sure everything is all right with the baby. We'll do a sonogram while we have you down in X-ray."

Jesse placed a call to the community phone booth, expecting to leave a message for the bishop and Gemma's family. On the second ring, someone answered. "Elmer Schultz speaking."

"Bishop Schultz, this is Jesse Crump."

"Jesse, we have been wondering what happened to you. Dale left a message saying you and Gemma Lapp were lost in the wilderness."

Jesse went on to explain the detour, the accident and admitted he was responsible for getting them lost in the woods. He assured the bishop that their injuries were only minor ones.

"I praise *Gott* it was not worse. What can I do to aid you?" the bishop asked.

"If you could arrange for our transportation home that would be great. And let Gemma's family know she is okay."

"I will as soon as I finish speaking with you."

Jesse hung up the phone. He eyed the vending machine in the corner. He strolled to it and noticed a package of beef jerky among the candy bars. He inserted the correct amount of change and enjoyed the snack even while he felt guilty that Gemma hadn't had anything to eat yet. For all his praise of pine bark, it hadn't satisfied his appetite.

He saw the nurse who had been with Gemma motion to him and he hurried to her side. "How is she?"

"I haven't heard a report on her X-ray yet. She's on her way back. You can wait in her room if you'd like."

"*Danki*, thank you," he said, forgetting for a moment that she wouldn't understand his Pennsylvania *Deitsh* language. The room was still empty when he stepped inside. He took a seat in one of the chairs pushed back against the wall.

The doctor came in and held open the door for the people moving Gemma. The doctor caught sight of him. "Mr. Lapp, you will be happy to know that your wife and baby are both doing fine. Her ankle is sprained but there are no broken bones."

"Bobbli?" Stunned, Jesse looked from the doctor to Gemma for an explanation. He spoke to her in Pennsylvania *Deitsh*, so the man wouldn't understand what they were saying. "Gemma, what is he talking about?"

She covered her face with her hands. "I'm sorry. I couldn't tell you. I am so ashamed," she replied in the same language.

"Then this is true. You're with child? You were baptized. You made a vow before the church and before God."

The doctor looked puzzled and concerned. "I don't understand what you are saying. The baby is fine now. As I told your wife, the condition she has will require a cesarean section, but with good prenatal care, both she and the child should come through with flying colors." He laid a hand on Gemma's shoulder. "Don't cry. You are worrying your husband."

Gemma turned her face to the wall.

Jesse found his voice. "I'm not her husband." He got up and walked out of the room.

In the hall, he stopped as a nurse pushed an elderly woman past him in a wheelchair. He raked a hand through his hair.

Gemma was pregnant. Who was the father?

Had she gotten married in Florida and left her husband? Or had she broken her vows to the church? Sadly, the latter was the most likely explanation. She wouldn't have needed to keep it a secret otherwise.

A cold sensation settled in the pit of his stomach. If that were the case, he knew exactly what lay in store for her and her baby. He was the child of an unwed mother.

* * *

Gemma kept her face averted through the first hour of the ride home. Jesse sat silently beside her. Dale had been released too. He sat up front with the driver, a woman the bishop had sent to pick them up. They would be home in another few hours.

"What are your plans?" Jesse asked quietly in *Deitsh* in case they should be overheard.

She glanced at him, but he was still staring out the window at the snow-covered landscape. At least he was speaking to her. Shame almost kept her silent, but she clutched at the olive branch he offered.

"I don't know," she replied quietly in their Amish language.

He turned to stare at her. "You must have some idea."

She kept her voice low, although she didn't think Dale or the driver understood what was being said. "Before the accident, I thought I could put the baby up for adoption. I have family in Pennsylvania that I could stay with. I'm sure there must be an Amish couple who would love to adopt a child in the area."

"And after the accident?"

She gripped her fingers tightly together. "I was worried that something might happen to him or her. For the first time, I started thinking that my mistake was actually my baby."

"The child is not to blame."

She cupped her hands over her abdomen. "I know that."

"Have you told the father?"

"I did."

"Did he offer to marry you?"

"*Nee.* His name was Robert Fisher. He left town the next day without telling me where he was going. I waited months for him to return. He never did. I have no idea how to contact him. I finally decided to come home."

"I would judge him to be a coward, but it is wrong to judge any man. Only God can know what is in the heart of the person."

There was nothing she could say about Robert that wouldn't make her sound bitter. Jesse looked out the window again. "Do you love him?"

She swallowed hard. "I thought so. He said he loved me. I believed him. I was very naive."

"Life gives the test first and then the lesson is learned."

She had failed the test miserably and couldn't offer anything in her own defense. She had wanted to be loved, but she had been tricked into believing Robert's love was real.

"When this becomes known in the community, you will be shunned unless you make a public confession to the church."

"I know." She dreaded telling her parents more than she dreaded telling everyone else.

"What did the doctor mean when he said you had a complication that would require a cesarean section?"

"He called it a placenta previa. It means the blood supply for the baby will tear open when labor starts." *Please, Lord, protect this child. I didn't want to be pregnant, but I would never wish harm to befall a baby. My baby. Have mercy, I beg You.*

"That is dangerous for the child and for you?"

She found it hard to speak past the lump in her throat. "He said it was. The nurse gave me a pamphlet to read about it."

"May I see it?"

Gemma frowned. Why would he want to read such a

thing? She withdrew it from her pocket and laid it on the seat between them rather than handing it to him. A baptized member of the faith was forbidden to accept anything from the hand of a shunned person, to eat at the same table or to do business with them. Jesse knew that.

He picked it up. "You aren't shunned yet, Gemma Lapp. That is for the church to decide."

He remained quiet for the next few minutes and then handed it back to her. "*Danki*. Will you be able to face the entire congregation and admit your mistakes?"

"I will have to, won't I? If I wish to remain in New Covenant as a member of the Amish faith."

"You could accept the shunning and live apart from the community or become English."

Gemma was surprised by his comment. "To face the shame I have brought to my family won't be easy for me or for them. I won't give up my faith, but it might be better if I moved away."

"You should consider what is best for the child, not only for you and your family."

"I don't know what's best, but I think I want to keep my baby, even if I have to raise him or her by myself. I hope my parents will understand and allow us to stay with them."

He nodded, but his eyes held a faraway look. "A fatherless child faces many hardships, as does a mother without a husband."

There was something in his voice that made her look at him closely. It wasn't a random comment, she was sure of it. "It sounds like you know someone in that position."

He fixed his gaze on her. "I do. My mother was never married."

Chapter Eight

Jesse watched Gemma's eyes widen with disbelief. "Your mother wasn't married?"

"I never knew my father. Not even his name. She never spoke of him."

"How awful. Why? I mean…if you don't mind telling me about it."

He hadn't told a single soul his story since coming to New Covenant, but he heard only sympathy in her voice. "I don't usually talk about it."

A wry smile tugged at the corner of her lips. "I used to think you didn't talk about much of anything. I was happy to discover I was wrong. If you don't feel like sharing, that is okay with me. I won't mention what you have told me to anyone. We are friends now and I value your friendship."

Gemma and her child were facing the same situation his mother had endured. He plucked at the dressing on his right hand, remembering some of the painful parts of his childhood. "My mother worked as a maid for an *Englisch* woman who lived near my grandfather's farm. My grandfather died shortly after I was born. We had no other family. My mother made a public confession and was forgiven. She attended church services, but we never stayed to eat or visit with other members. She avoided people and made sure I did too."

He fell silent as he recalled the day he had asked her why he didn't have a father like the other children. Her answer had frightened him.

She grabbed him by the shoulders, shook him and told him never to ask about his father again. He never had.

Gemma laid her hand on his arm. "That sounds like a lonely existence."

"It was."

"How sad for her and for you."

"It wasn't much better when I started school. I was shy. I didn't know how to act around others. I had trouble learning to read. I was bigger than the other *kinder* my age but not as smart. I tried to keep to myself, but I was teased a lot. They called me Jesse the Ox. The name stuck with me until I moved here."

"Children don't realize how much words can hurt." She looked down at her clasped hands. "I am guilty of using hurtful words."

"Something tells me you have seen the error of your ways," he said softly.

"I hope I have. I'm ashamed of the way I behaved toward you last year."

He shrugged. "I wasn't always kind to you either."

"Thank you for confiding in me, Jesse."

"Your decision will have a long-lasting impact on your child. Make it carefully." Because a child growing up without his or her father's name could feel like an outcast even if he or she wasn't.

"How am I to know what's best for this baby?"

"I reckon you pray on it."

She turned to stare out the window, and they made the rest of the journey in silence.

It was almost dark by the time they arrived at the bishop's business. Jesse was surprised to see the large number of horses and buggies filling the parking lot.

Dale turned around. "It looks like we have a welcoming committee. I guess everyone has heard about our adventure by now."

Their driver pulled the vehicle to a stop in the driveway. The bishop opened the front door, letting the cold evening air pour in. "Welcome back, Dale Kaufman. I'm right glad to have my best hauler returned. You'll have your job waiting for you when you are able to start driving again."

While the bishop spoke with Dale, the door beside Jesse opened and his friend Michael Shetler reached in and grabbed Jesse's uninjured hand. "It's good to see you in one piece. You were found before we even knew you were lost, my friend. God moves in mysterious ways for sure. He spared us a lot of grief and worry."

Michael's dog, Sadie, pressed in to nuzzle Jesse's hand. A yellow Lab mix, she was Michael's constant companion and helped to warn him of the PTSD flashbacks he sometimes had. Jesse patted her head. She was pushed aside by Jesse's dog, Roscoe, a shaggy black-and-white mutt who had shown up at his door last spring. Jesse smiled as he took the dog's head between his hands. "Hello, big fella. I missed you too. Who has been feeding you?"

Michael grinned. "I have. He showed up looking

hungry the first night you were gone. I took care of your stock too."

Michael leaned lower to look inside the car. "I'm mighty glad to see you too, Gemma. Bethany wanted to come but I told her she should wait in a warm house and hear all about it from you tomorrow."

"*Danki*, Michael. Tell her I will come by first thing tomorrow morning."

The door beside her opened. Her father stood waiting for her to get out with a big grin on his face. "*Gott* is good to me. He has brought my daughter home."

Gemma immediately burst into tears. She scrambled out of the car and into her father's embrace. He patted her back awkwardly. "There, there. You are safe now. It's all over. Come, I will get you home to your mother and the two of you can have a good cry together. She sent along your winter coat so you wouldn't catch a chill." He held it out to her.

Gemma took it but kept it bundled in front of her rather than putting it on.

Jesse got out and was soon surrounded by the men of the community, who plied him with questions about the ordeal. He answered them as best he could while he made his way toward the Lapps' buggy. He wanted to speak to Gemma before she left. She was already seated inside when he reached it. She managed to quell her sniffles long enough to extend her hand to him. "Thank you for everything."

He squeezed her hand in reply. "All I did was get us lost. If I can do anything for you, just ask."

She pulled her hand free and looked away. "That means a lot to me, Jesse, *danki*."

He shrugged. "You were a *goot* companion, except when you were scolding me."

"I should promise never to scold you again, but I fear I wouldn't be able to keep it. Stay safe."

He gazed into her eyes, wishing they wouldn't drift apart but he knew they would. She had her friends and her family. They would take care of her. His job was done.

Gemma's father wiped his eyes with the back of his hand. "You have my gratitude and that of her mother for taking care of our Gemma. She was blessed to have you looking after her." He shook Jesse's hand, climbed into the buggy and drove away.

Jesse watched it disappear down the road. He was going to miss Gemma. That they might never be alone again, might never enjoy the comfort of each other's company again hit him hard. She had a rough journey ahead of her. He wouldn't be able to protect her and her baby.

Michael slapped Jesse on the shoulder. "The bishop has invited us inside for coffee. Come on. We all have questions for you."

Jesse followed Michael inside the front office of the business. Both dogs tried to follow them, but Jesse told Roscoe to stay and Michael said the same to Sadie. It was warmer inside the building. Men began removing their coats. A few chairs lined the plain gray walls. One had been saved for him. Samples of shed materials took up shelf space on one wall. The place smelled of saw-dust and paint.

"Why didn't you stay in the truck? That's what I would've done." Ivan, Michael's teenage brother-in-law, offered his opinion.

"That was supposed to be the plan," Dale said. "So why didn't you stay there?"

"The gas tank had a leak. We couldn't run the heater for fear of starting a fire." He explained the rest of their adventure, including his mistake of losing the trail.

Michael punched Jesse's shoulder. "It couldn't have been easy being snowed in with Gemma Lapp." Everyone but Jesse laughed.

The bishop handed Jesse a cup of coffee. He wrapped his fingers around the warm thick white mug. "She was no trouble."

"You're just being kind," Michael said. "I know how much of a pest she was in the past."

Jesse stared at the dark coffee in his cup and thought about Gemma's rose hip tea. He might even miss that. "She has changed."

There were more questions and suggestions for surviving a blizzard from some of the older men. Ivan asked Jesse to teach him how to make rabbit snares. Jesse looked around and realized how thankful he was to be surrounded by friends who appreciated him for his skills and didn't poke fun at him because of his size, except in a friendly way.

"Who bought that eighty acres at auction?" he asked when he had a chance.

"Leroy Lapp did," Michael said. "He got it for a steal."

Jesse managed a wry smile. "Because I wasn't there to bid against him." Gemma's father was a good farmer. He would make the most of the property.

Jesse's plans to expand his farm would have to wait. It was a bitter disappointment, but he accepted it as God's will. One by one, the crowd of men headed for home until only Jesse and the bishop were left in the small office. The bishop took Jesse's empty mug from his hand. "You must be tired. Let me take you home."

Jesse shook his head. "It's not far. I feel the need to walk."

The bishop was a keen man, sensitive to the needs of others. "Is there something on your mind? Is something troubling you?"

Jesse shook his head. He would respect Gemma's privacy and allow her to decide if and when she should confide in the bishop. "*Nee*, good night, Bishop Schultz. I will be in to work tomorrow morning."

"*Goot.* We have many orders to fill."

Jesse walked out of the building. Roscoe was waiting outside the door. He trotted ahead a short distance but came back and barked once. Jesse paused to pet him. Happy with the attention, Roscoe fell into step beside Jesse as they followed a gravel road leading south.

The night was clear, and the stars were beginning to come out. New Covenant had received six inches of new snow, but they had been spared the brunt of the blizzard. The snow and gravel crunched beneath his boots as he walked along with his head down and his hands in his coat pockets. The doctor had warned him that his hand would ache as it was healing, and he was right. But it wasn't his discomfort that occupied his mind.

Gemma was in trouble. "It has nothing to do with me. I kept her safe when she needed me and now she is with her family." Roscoe perked up his ears.

Jesse glanced at his dog. "My responsibility has ended, right?"

He wanted to believe it was true, but he couldn't shake the feeling that she still needed him. They had become close during their time together. He had seen a side of her he hadn't known existed. She had endurance, a sense of humor, a level head. She was a quick thinker. If she hadn't remembered the dead cedar tree, the search plane might've been too far away to see the signal fire by the time he thought of it. She had promised that she wouldn't whine, and she hadn't. She had endured pain and bone-chilling cold without a whimper.

He stopped in the middle of the road. "Why am I listing her good qualities to myself?"

Roscoe sat with his tail wagging slowly and his gaze pinned to Jesse's face. Jesse sighed. "I'll tell you why. Because those are the qualities I hope to find in a wife someday. And that is a ridiculous thought. As odd as it sounds, Gemma and I have become friends."

Still, the nagging feeling that she needed him wouldn't go away. He stared off into the distance until Roscoe whined again. Jesse patted him and resumed walking. There was nothing he could do for Gemma and her baby. He had to accept that.

Chapter Nine

Gemma sat silently beside her father in their buggy as he drove home. The moment she dreaded was fast approaching and she wasn't sure she could go through with it.

"Are you all right, daughter?"

She started to say she was fine but remembered how much Jesse disliked her use of the word instead of an honest reply. "I'm tired, and my foot aches."

"We will be home soon. Tonight, you can rest easy in your own bed."

"That sounds *wunderbar*." If only she could put off telling her parents about her condition until another time. But doing so would only make it harder.

Gemma stared out the window and saw they were approaching Bethany and Michael's house. Bethany stood at the front door. She waved when the buggy drew close enough. Gemma waved back. There was so much she needed to tell her friend. She needed Bethany's advice and her support. Hopefully she would remain a friend after she learned of Gemma's transgression.

The buggy rolled on and Gemma's home came into

view. The tall two-story house, painted white with black shutters, looked inviting with lamplight shining from the windows. Her mother's beautiful flower garden was covered with snow, but she had colorful bird feeders arranged where she could view them from her kitchen window. The big red barn with white trim looked immaculate against the snowy backdrop.

"It's good to be home," she said quietly and realized it was true. She had never appreciated the love and care her parents lavished on their property. The work of tending the flowers, caring for the animals, even painting the barn had seemed like tedious chores. Now she hoped she could do those things again, only this time it would be with a glad heart if her parents allowed her to stay.

Her mother came rushing out of the house when her father stopped the buggy by the front gate. Gemma got down and was immediately embraced by her mother. Gemma kept the coat between them, not wanting her mother to notice her condition. Tears stung Gemma's eyes, but she refused to let them fall. There would be time for tears later.

"It's so *goot* to have you home at last. Come in out of the cold," her mother said as she slipped her arm around Gemma's shoulders and began shepherding her to the front door. Inside the warm house, the familiar smells of home bombarded Gemma. Her mother had been baking. The smell of bread, fresh from the oven, dominated the air but under that, she could smell the scent of cooking chicken, her mother's pine cleaner and the lemon polish she used on the furniture.

"Let me take your cloak."

Gemma handed it over, feeling self-conscious about her growing figure. Her mother didn't seem to notice the change beneath her loose dress. They went into the kitchen, where her mother began fixing a cup of tea for each of them. She had chicken noodle soup cooking on the stove. "Supper is almost ready."

"I've missed your cooking." Gemma took a seat at the table and listened to her mother's happy chatter. Before long, she was up to speed on the inhabitants of New Covenant. Her mother was one who enjoyed gossip and was happy to share what she knew.

Gemma's father came in, stomping the snow from his boots on the porch before stepping inside. He unbuckled his overshoes and pulled them off. He set them on a large tray meant to catch the melting snow beside the door. "It's going to get cold again. My arthritis tells me we're in for a long winter."

"You should have chopped more wood before now," her mother said. "We will run low by next month."

Her father shrugged. "I will have Jesse help me cut and haul some in. He's always glad to lend a helping hand."

Gemma took a sip of tea from the cup her mother handed her. She set it down carefully and waited until her mother served up bowls of hearty soup loaded with vegetables, tender chicken and her homemade egg noodles. A plate held warm mini loaves of bread and a crock of fresh butter. It was the best meal Gemma had eaten in her life despite her nervousness.

When the supper dishes were cleared and her father had refilled his coffee cup, she said, "Please sit down, *Mamm.* I have something to tell you both."

"What is this news?" her mother asked over her shoulder as she rinsed the last plate.

"Come sit down, *Mamm.*"

"I can listen standing up."

Gemma bowed her head. "I'm so sorry about this. I didn't know what else to do, so I came home." She looked up to see her mother's puzzled expression slowly change to disbelief. She stopped drying her hands at the sink.

She met Gemma's gazed for a long moment, then tears filled her eyes. "Oh, *nee.*"

Her father stared between the two of them with an expression of confusion. "Oh, what? Why are you crying, *Mudder*?"

"Because I'm going to have a baby." Gemma covered her face with her hands as tears slipped down her cheeks.

"I don't believe it," he declared. "My daughter would not behave in such a wanton fashion."

"I'm sorry, *Daed*. It's true. I thought he loved me and that we would marry, but he left and never came back."

"Who is he? I'll speak to his father and see that he makes this right."

"I don't know who his father is. He told me his family was from Ohio and that's all he told me. I have no idea how to find him."

Her father's face grew red. "Gemma, how could you disregard the teaching of the church? I don't know what to say. How can I hold my head up among the congregation? I am a minister now. I oversee the flock along with the bishop. I will become a laughingstock, a preacher who couldn't raise his own daughter to be chaste."

She shrank from his words. It was what she had expected, what she deserved, but it was still painful.

"Hush, husband. This isn't about you," *Mamm* said quietly when she had composed herself. "This is our child, and she is in trouble."

Gemma wanted to throw herself into her mother's comforting arms.

He rounded on his wife. "Are you not ashamed of her? How will you hold your head up in church when this becomes known?"

"Church is not a place to hold up your head. It is a place to bow low before God."

Some of the bluster left her father's face. Gemma was grateful for her mother's intervention. "I know I have shamed you. I am truly sorry."

Her mother folded her hands together on the table. "Is this the same young man you were seeing in Florida?"

Gemma nodded.

"I thought he was an Amish boy." Her father's frown was back.

"He is Amish, but he had not been baptized."

Daed shook a finger at Gemma. "You have been. You should have known better. And don't tell me I'm wrong, wife."

"You are not wrong, but spilled milk can't be put back in the glass. Many a young woman has lost her common sense in the heat of the moment. It isn't an excuse, but it happens. We must decide what to do now."

"We won't have any success getting someone from here to marry her when word gets out. I'll have my brother in Lancaster find a fellow. There must be some man who will marry her once he learns he will inherit this farm one day."

Gemma stared at her clasped hands. "I don't need a husband."

"What do you want to do, Gemma?" *Mamm* asked gently.

"At first, I thought I could go and stay with Cousin

Shelia or Cousin Donna May and give the child up for adoption when the time came."

"*Ja*, that is a *goot* plan," *Daed* said. "That way, no one has to know about this."

Mamm scowled at him. "You would give away your grandson or granddaughter before you have even looked upon the child's face? Have I married such a heartless man?"

"I don't want to give up my baby anymore. I want to raise my child myself." Gemma glanced between her parents, hoping they would understand.

Her father shook his head. "We have given you everything you ever wanted, Gemma, and this is how you repay us—by bringing shame on our heads. *Nee*. You will not live in my home as an unwed mother. You will marry. I will arrange something as quickly as possible."

"*Nee, Daed*, please. I don't wish to marry." The thought of it made her sick.

He silenced her with a stern look. "There will still be talk when the child arrives early, but having a husband will provide some protection for you and the child from gossip. You will make a private confession to the bishop as soon as possible. I'm finished talking." He rose to his feet and left the room.

Gemma turned to her mother. "He can't make me marry someone I don't know."

"This seems harsh, but I have to agree with him. With a husband, you and your babe will have security. Affection can grow between two people who respect each other and work together for the good of the family."

"I'm not looking for love. It may exist for others but not for me. Not anymore."

"It may feel like that now, but time has a way of healing our hurts."

"There is something else you need to know. The doctor said I will need a hospital delivery. I have something called placenta previa."

Her mother's eyes widened. "I know of this condition. We should ask the midwife in to see you soon. She will know how best to care for you."

Mamm leaned back in her chair. "Finish your tea, Gemma. We will talk more about this in the morning."

Gemma nodded but knew this had only been the first hurdle on her journey. Which way the road led from here was known only to God.

After praying for guidance, something she had rarely done since leaving home, Gemma crawled beneath the heavy quilts she and her mother had made together. Her eyes burned from weeping, and her heart ached worse than her ankle. Snug and warm in a soft bed for the first time in days, she lay curled on her side in a state of half waking. Uncertainty kept her awake. Was she being selfish, wanting to keep her child? Wouldn't it be better to give her babe a mother and a father? Could she marry a man she didn't know? What if they didn't get along? She shivered at the thought. Finally she fell asleep without reaching any decisions.

She rose early the next morning and went downstairs. She found her parents both at the kitchen table. They appeared tired and worn. She wasn't the only one wrestling with the future.

Daed wouldn't meet her eyes and Gemma's heart sank at his cold expression. He rose and walked to the kitchen window. "Someone just drove in."

"Who is it?" *Mamm* got up to put a kettle of water back on to heat.

"I think it's Jesse."

"What is he doing here?" *Mamm* looked at Gemma.

"I have no idea," Gemma said, wondering the same thing.

Jesse entered the house and saw Gemma's father scowling at him. "This isn't a good time to visit, Jesse. Can it not wait until tomorrow?"

"Maybe it could, but I would rather do it now. I have some business I'd like to discuss." He'd spent a restless night worrying about Gemma and her family's reaction. He needed to see how she was getting along.

Gemma's father gestured toward the living room. "Come in and have a seat. Would you like some coffee?"

Jesse shook his head. "I'd like to speak to Gemma for a minute, if you don't mind."

Her parents looked puzzled but got up and left the room.

Gemma leaned toward him. "What are you doing here?" she asked in a small whisper. She looked pale, tired and on the verge of tears.

"I wanted to see how you are feeling. Have you told them?"

"I did." She kept her face down. He wished she would look at him. He wanted to see her eyes.

"And?"

"*Daed* was upset. *Mamm* was sad and disappointed, but she didn't judge me harshly."

"The hard part is over, then. Have you decided what you are going to do?"

"Father wants to arrange a marriage for me to help quiet the scandal. He's going to have his brother in

Lancaster find someone willing to wed me. He is offering to let some fine fellow inherit this farm if he agrees. Apparently gaining good farmland can offset having a sullied wife."

That Leroy was willing to go to such lengths surprised him. "I see. Do you wish to marry?"

"*Nee.* I don't want to spend my life with some stranger. I want to keep my baby, but *Daed* says I can't live in his house as an unwed mother. I've been thinking I might go to live with one of my cousins until the baby is born. Then I will try to resume my life somewhere."

"Somewhere but not here?"

She shook her head still without looking at him. "I don't think I can stay here. My folks will always know what I've done."

"You made a mistake, Gemma. You have to forgive yourself too."

"Perhaps in time." Finally she looked up at him. "Only…"

"Only what?"

A tear slipped down her cheek. "Only I don't want to move away from my family and my friends, and I don't want to marry someone who only wants my father's land. What shall I do?"

He wanted to draw her into his arms and comfort her, but he knew such action wasn't proper. "I don't know the answer. I wish I did."

She wiped her cheek and drew a deep breath. "It isn't fair of me to ask you. This is my problem. I'll solve it. What business do you have with my father?"

"He bought the land I wanted at the auction I missed. I came to see if he'd be willing to sell it to me for a small profit."

"I hope he will. You missed your chance to buy it because you stayed with me."

"*Gott* allowed it. He must have something else in mind for me."

She laid a hand on her abdomen. "I wish I knew what he had in mind for us."

He gestured toward her foot. "You should go put your foot up so the swelling doesn't come back."

She sent him a tiny smile. "Is that your way of getting rid of me?"

"I thought it was kinder than saying you look worn-out. If we were back in the cabin, I'd tell you to go lie down."

She rose to her feet. "If we were back in the cabin, I'd tell you to go eat bark."

He grinned. "I can bring some over for you later."

Waving her hand, she declined. "I think not. A nap sounds much more appetizing. Thanks for coming to check on me."

"Isn't that what friends do?"

She smiled and nodded. He watched her leave, limping slightly, and then went in to speak with her father.

Leroy was seated in his blue overstuffed chair with his feet on a matching ottoman. Gemma's mother was on the sofa. She rose and left the room without speaking.

Jesse took a seat in a straight-backed chair close to Leroy. "I heard you bought the land that borders mine."

"You heard right. It's a fine piece of ground."

"I thought so too. I had hoped to get in my bid but that didn't happen. Would you be interested in selling it to me? I'm willing to see you make a profit on it."

Leroy ran a hand down his beard. "I can see why you'd want it. Let me think it over."

"Fair enough. That's all I can ask." Jesse rose to his feet to leave.

"Before you go, let me ask you something."

"Sure."

It took Leroy a moment to phrase his question. "A year and a half ago Gemma embarrassed you with unwanted attention. She embarrassed us, as well. Be honest with me. Did she continue that when you were together?"

Jesse shook his head. "She didn't. She was considerate, uncomplaining and worked hard to make the best of a bad situation. No one could fault her behavior. In fact, I came to admire her spirit."

"I'm glad to hear you aren't disgusted with her anymore."

"She has changed a great deal."

Leroy frowned. "More than you know."

Jesse hesitated. He didn't think Gemma had told her parents he knew her secret, but he thought Leroy deserved to know. "I'm aware of Gemma's condition."

"You are?" Leroy seemed to sink into his chair. "How many other people know?"

"Only me. I won't say anything."

Sighing heavily, Leroy glanced at the door his wife had gone through. "It will come out sooner or later. As you might imagine, my wife is heartbroken. We are struggling to know what to do and praying *Gott* shows us the best way to help our daughter. I will speak with the bishop today."

"He is a *goot* man. He will give you sound advice. I should get going. I told him I'd be in to work today."

"Let him know I'll be in later."

Jesse nodded, put on his hat and left. Outside, he

opened the door of his buggy and looked over his shoulder at the house. He saw Gemma standing at a window upstairs. He raised his hand in a brief wave. She opened the window and leaned out. "Did he sell it to you?"

"He's thinking about it."

"At least he didn't say no." She closed the window and waved, but she looked sad and lonely. She turned away and once again he was left with the feeling that he should do something to help her.

Her parents were out when Gemma came downstairs. She pulled on her old coat and boots and headed toward Bethany's house, using a stout stick to help her walk. She prayed her friend would be home and the children would be already gone.

Ivan and Jenny were Bethany's younger brother and sister. The responsibility for raising them had fallen to her after the deaths of their mother and later their grandfather. It was Bethany's grandfather who had founded the community of New Covenant. Bethany had been determined to raise the children on her own and continue his dream of a new Amish settlement far from the tourists in Pennsylvania. Then Michael Shetler arrived to take over her grandfather's business. It wasn't long before Bethany and Michael fell in love and were married. Now they were expecting their first child. Bethany was Gemma's dearest friend. She knew she would find comfort and compassion there.

Gemma knocked on her door a short time later. Bethany opened the door wide, grinning from ear to ear. "I was hoping you would come early. Michael left a few minutes ago to see about fixing a clock at someone's home." Bethany grabbed Gemma and gave her a hug.

"Promise me you are back for good. I've missed you so much. Tell me everything you have been doing."

"I will tell you everything, but it is not what you expect. Do you have some coffee made? This is going to take a while."

"I have coffee and rolls waiting for you inside. We are holding Sunday services here for the first time. I hope you can give me a hand getting ready. There is so much to do."

It was wonderful to feel welcomed and needed. "Of course I will."

Coffee cups in hand, the two women sat at the table in Bethany's homey kitchen and Gemma laid out the whole sad story of her time in Florida and the trip home. She told her friend everything, including her father's plan to find her a husband.

"My life keeps getting more complicated, Bethany. What should I do?" She waited for Bethany's advice.

Bethany slowly shook her head as she stirred a spoon of sugar into her coffee and started pulling apart a cinnamon bread stick. "Gemma, I can't tell you what to do. I wish I could."

"What good is a friend who won't advise me?" Gemma sipped a cup of strong coffee and prayed it would stay down.

"A real friend helps you see your choices. They don't make those choices for you."

"You sound like Jesse." She took a bite of a saltine cracker.

"My heart bleeds for the position you are in. You know that, don't you? I love the child I carry more each day. I look forward to the birth of my baby as a wondrous event. That you are unable to share the same joy I feel breaks my heart. A baby is a great gift from God."

Gemma reached across the table to lay a hand on Bethany's arm. "I'm happy for you. Please believe that. You deserve the joy a baby will bring you and Michael."

"You deserve that joy too."

"I'm afraid I may find sorrow instead of happiness."

"Why?"

"I didn't want this child in the beginning. I didn't want to be pregnant. But I want it now. I do. I want to hold and love my baby, but I'm afraid. What if *Gott* takes my babe back to heaven?"

Bethany leaned across the table and took Gemma's hands in hers. "Every mother has that fear, but to worry is to doubt *Gott*'s mercy. He will help you bear whatever comes into your life if you open your heart to His love."

Gemma squeezed Bethany's hands. "I know. I'm trying to have faith."

"Have you spoken to the bishop?"

"Not yet."

Bethany smiled gently. "You will be forgiven. You know that, don't you?"

"People forgive, but they don't forget." Gemma shivered inwardly.

"They will in time."

"I have shamed my parents. I can never forget that. I know my father won't. He can barely stand to look at me. I believe it may be best for me to go away."

"A new baby can warm the coldest heart. You'll see."

"Oh, Bethany, I pray you are right."

Chapter Ten

There were two buggies parked in front of the house when Gemma returned home. She recognized both. One belonged to the bishop. The other one was her father's. He was home from work early.

Her parents weren't wasting any time. She drew a deep breath and went in to face them.

They were all seated in the living room. There was a platter of cookies on the end table. They all had cups of coffee in their hands. The bishop wore a stern expression she had never seen before. His wife, Myra, sat beside him with a kindly smile for Gemma. Her parents sat with bowed heads.

She lowered her eyes. "Good morning, Bishop. I trust you are well?"

"I'm in good health, but I am greatly distressed over the reason for my visit today."

"I'm very sorry for the pain I've caused my family and you."

"I believe you, child. Come in and sit down."

Gemma took the only seat left to her, the one directly

facing the bishop. "Would you care for some coffee?" her mother asked.

Gemma shook her head. "I had coffee with Bethany this morning."

"I'm glad you have a friend you can confide in," the bishop said. Gemma wondered how he knew she had told Bethany about her pregnancy.

Her father cleared his throat. "I asked the bishop to hear your confession."

This wasn't what she had been expecting. "I thought only minor offenses were handled in private confessions. I assumed I would have to make a public confession in front of all our baptized members at a *sitz gma.*" The *sitting church* was a special meeting held after the Sunday worship was over where only baptized members of the congregation participated. A punishment was chosen if all members agreed. Gemma was prepared to be shunned for a month or more before being accepted back into the church.

Bishop Shultz nodded once. "That is normally the case. While you have committed a grave offense, it is not a matter that has drawn the attention of the whole congregation, and therefore I don't feel it needs to be resolved publicly at a member's meeting. It is your father's understanding that you have repented and wish to once again join our fellowship."

"That is true. I do repent."

"Then begin."

She clasped her hands together and lowered her gaze. She had learned the words of confession in her baptismal classes several years ago but never thought back then that she would have to actually utter the words. "I confess that I failed to uphold my vow. I want to make peace with God and the church, and I promise to do better in the future."

"Come forward and accept the kiss of peace." His wife came to stand beside him as he beckoned to Gemma.

She stood and walked forward. Myra laid her hands on Gemma's shoulders and kissed her on each cheek. "Welcome once again into the house of the faithful."

A second later, she was embraced by her mother. Her father walked away without a word.

Gemma couldn't believe it was over so quickly.

The bishop glanced from her father's retreating figure to Gemma. "Remember that we are only human and none of us are without blemish. Your father wishes for you to take a husband. I agree it is best for a child to have both a mother and a father to nurture and guide him or her."

She thought of Jesse and his story about his unhappy childhood. Would she subject her child to the same unhappiness by staying single? What was the right thing to do? She sighed. "What man wants to marry a wife who doesn't love him? How can that be a loving home?"

The bishop smiled gently. "My grandmother had an illegitimate child and married my grandfather a year later. She told me she barely knew him before their wedding day, but she had faith in her father's choice and faith in *Gott*. I remember them as a happy couple who loved all eight of their children and all twenty-five of their grandchildren. Sometimes we must take things on faith."

Gemma's mother remained with her as her father returned to walk the bishop and his wife out.

"Do you feel better?" her mother asked as she took a seat in the chair.

All was forgiven. It was something Gemma had heard her entire life, but it was the first time she had experienced it. Her spirits rose. "I do feel better, but I wish *Daed* could forgive me."

"He has."

"I'm not so sure. He's barely spoken to me."

"He loves you, but he is struggling to see the path *Gott* wants him to take. Give him some time. Michael and Bethany are hosting the Sunday service. I'm sure Bethany could use an extra hand getting things ready."

"I have already told her that I'll help," Gemma answered softly.

"We'll go over together first thing tomorrow." Her mother looked as if she wanted to say more but left the room with only a backward glance.

Gemma sank onto the sofa. The two things she had been dreading the most had come and gone. All the energy she had spent worrying about telling her parents and telling the bishop left her feeling limp. She was forgiven. She would try hard to become a demure and humble person worthy of the forgiveness that had been shown her.

Getting ready to host church services meant deep cleaning for the home owner inside and out. No room or nook was spared. Because of the large amount of work involved, each family was expected to host the bimonthly meeting only once a year if the congregation was large enough.

Gemma and her mother were getting out of their buggy at Bethany's just as Gemma's cousin Anna Miller arrived in a pony cart. Gemma and Anna had been friends from the cradle and quickly greeted each other with a hug. "Say you are home for good, cousin. It wasn't as much fun without you."

Gemma drew back, suddenly worried how Anna would receive her news. "I have something I must tell you."

Anna squeezed Gemma's hand. "I already know. Bethany told me. I hope you don't mind. I knew something was troubling her and I pressured her until she confided in me. A sin that is forgiven should not be mentioned again and we will not." She laid a hand on Gemma's stomach. "Another baby is coming into the world, and that is a reason for joy."

"*Danki*. I never expected people to be so accepting. I'm humbled by it."

"Not everyone will be. There are some people who will condemn privately before they forgive publicly. Just remember, you have family and friends to support you."

"Friends, but not all of my family. My father isn't speaking to me. He wants me to marry. He's willing to offer his farm as an incentive if it will bring someone willing to wed me."

"His farm? He can't be serious?" Anna looked outraged.

"He won't give it up while he's alive, but he'll leave it to my husband in his will."

"Your father will come around. There is much work to do. Let's get started."

Inside the house, the women gathered around the kitchen table, each one setting her basket on it. Gemma opened the lid of the one she carried and began to pull out its contents. "I brought a few things." She produced cleaning supplies, plastic pails, pine cleaner, rags, sponges and brushes.

"Where shall we start?" Anna asked.

Her mother picked up the pail and carried it to the sink. "I will finish these windows. Where is Jenny?"

"In school," Bethany said. "She'll be home about four." Bethany's sister was ten years old and always a willing helper.

"I'll get this food put away." Anna opened her basket and brought out two loaves of bread and a cherry pie with a gorgeous golden lattice crust. Gemma felt her stomach rumble. Her morning sickness had subsided and her appetite seemed to be making up for lost time.

Next, Anna began unpacking china and flatware that would be needed to feed all fifty church members, along with four coffee cakes. "One for later when we need an energy boost and three for the church meal so you don't have to bake tonight."

Bethany was clearly overwhelmed by her kindness. "*Danki*. This is far too much."

"No thanks are needed. You will do the same when it is my turn to host the service," Anna assured her.

"I will," Bethany agreed.

"What do you need me to do?" Gemma asked, looking over the kitchen.

Bethany took a second to gather her thoughts. "Anna, if you want to start in the living room that would be great. Gemma, perhaps you could help me drag the mattresses outside so I can beat the dust out of them."

Gemma's mother shook her head. "None of you pregnant girls are going to be struggling with heavy mattresses. Leroy and Jesse will be here after work. They will do the heavy lifting."

Gemma couldn't help the little jolt of happiness that shot through her when she realized she was going to see Jesse again today. She thought she would have to wait until Sunday.

The house quickly became a beehive of activity. Walls, floors and appliances were scrubbed until they shone. Windows sparkled and window curtains were washed. Everywhere inside the house, the sharp scent of pine cleaner filled the air.

Bethany stopped beside Gemma, who was polishing the hall table. "Can you believe it? In one morning, these women managed to do more inside the house than I could have accomplished in four days on my own."

"Many hands make light work." A sharp pain in her abdomen made Gemma grimace and bend over. She waited for it to come again, but it didn't. It was a reminder that her pregnancy wasn't going to be a normal one. "Be good, little one. Don't scare me like that."

"Are you okay?" Bethany asked.

Gemma managed a little smile. "I'm fine."

Bethany pointed to the couch. "Sit and take it easy."

"Only if you do."

Bethany plopped down and patted the cushion. "This is me resting. Now, you."

Gemma joined her for ten minutes and then both of them got back to work.

One of Michael's heirloom clocks on the mantel was striking four o'clock when all the women gathered in the kitchen once more. Bethany wiped her forehead with the back of her sleeve. "I don't know about you, but I've worked up an appetite. I believe I will sample the cherry pie. Would anyone else care for a piece?" The coffee cake had vanished before noon.

Mamm smiled brightly. "I thought you'd never ask."

"I'll get the plates?" Gemma was already moving toward the cabinets.

Bethany turned to Anna. "Would you like some?"

"Are you joking? I could eat the whole thing."

Mamm chuckled. "That's because you are eating for two."

Bethany and Anna shared a grin as Anna said, "That's what I keep telling my husband when he makes faces at my overflowing plate."

"Me too," Bethany said and giggled.

Gemma endured a stab of wistful envy. They had loving husbands to share their journeys into parenthood. She would travel that path alone unless she agreed to her father's plan. Was God leading her in that direction?

Marrying would allow her to keep her baby and remain near her parents and her friends. Agreeing to wed would lessen her father's displeasure. Would it be worth the trade-off? It was difficult to know what was best. The babe wasn't to blame but he or she would be a constant reminder of Gemma's fall from grace. For both Gemma and the man who wedded her.

Bethany and Anna were so happy about their pregnancies. Gemma wanted to feel that excitement, but she was afraid she never would.

Jesse stepped into Michael's house and heard the chatter of women pouring out of the kitchen. Jesse was happy to see Gemma in the midst of them. It appeared that she was fitting back into the community. Her friends had rallied around her. He was happy for her. There would be people who avoided her or spoke unkindly, but that would pass with time. Then he noticed she was standing a little apart from the group with her eyes downcast. There was something in her demeanor that seemed wrong.

She caught sight of him and smiled. His heart gave a happy leap. He had missed her companionship since returning to New Covenant. Finding time alone with her might not be easy but he was willing to try. Had she missed him? The hope that she had died a quick death.

Why should she? She was back among friends and family.

When they had been alone together in the wilderness, it was clear that she needed him. He knew what to do. How to take care of her. He knew how to find food and make a snug shelter. She didn't need any of that now.

He jumped when Michael patted him on the shoulder. "Hey, big guy. You're one for keeping secrets."

Jesse frowned. Did Michael know about Gemma's pregnancy? "I don't know what you're talking about."

"I see you making eyes at Gemma Lapp."

"I wasn't making eyes at her."

"Looked that way to me. You used to say she was annoying."

Jesse smiled. "She still can be."

"So, what is the story?"

"We are friends, nothing more."

"Friends?" Michael's eyebrows shot up.

Jesse scowled at him. "Is there something wrong with being Gemma's friend?"

Michael held up both hands. "*Nee*, not at all. I see my wife wants me." Jesse thought he heard Michael chuckle under his breath as he walked away.

"What are you mad about?" Gemma asked as she crossed the room.

"Michael was giving me a hard time."

"About what?"

"It's not important. What can I do to help?"

"You can help me hang the curtains up. You won't need a step stool."

"Lead on."

Gemma threaded the curtain rods through the pockets of the pale blue sheers and then gave them to Jesse. "How have you been?"

He hung them with ease. "Fine."

She chuckled. "I thought we weren't to use the word *fine*."

"You can't. I can."

"How is that fair?"

"I'll think of a reason in a minute."

Shaking her head, she handed him the next set of curtains. "I've missed you, Jesse."

He paused with the rod in his hands. "You have?"

"Is that so surprising?"

"*Ja*, it is."

"I just feel like I can be myself with you."

He hung the curtain and they moved to the next window in the living room. Everyone else was in the kitchen. "Who are you being the rest of the time?"

"The disappointing daughter. The confused mother-bride-to-be. The waffling woman."

He crossed his arms over his chest and gave her a stern look. "Aren't you being hard on yourself? You have some difficult decisions to make."

"The bishop agrees that I should marry for the baby's sake."

"But you don't think so."

She gazed at him intently. "What do you wish your mother had done?"

"I wish she had found happiness in life instead of hiding from it."

Gemma laid a hand on his arm. "I wish I could have known you as a boy. I would have been your friend."

"That you are my friend now is enough." He turned back to the window, afraid to say more. He had grown to care for her more than he'd realized.

She handed him another rod. "Last one."

He hung it up. "Now what?"

She dusted her hands together. "Now we wait to see how things go on Sunday."

"Are you ready to face everyone?"

"Absolutely...not."

He tapped her nose with one finger. "You will be fine. If you are done with me, your father said he wants to talk to me about that property."

She smiled brightly. "He must be going to sell it to you. That would be—"

"Fine," he answered with a smile to match hers, and they both laughed.

Jesse left Michael's home with a bounce in his step. He had a feeling that Gemma was right and her father was going to sell him the land. He wouldn't overpay for it. He hoped Leroy would ask a fair price.

When he reached the Lapp place, he saw Leroy putting shoes on one of his buggy horses by the barn. His pair of dapple-gray draft horses looked on over the corral fence. Jesse walked up beside Leroy and waited until he had finished driving in the last nail.

He put the horse's foot down and straightened. "Thanks for coming by, Jesse."

"Can I give you a hand?"

"Nope, this is the last shoe. I wanted to speak to you about that property you are interested in."

"I'm willing to pay you a fair price."

"How does free and clear sound?"

Puzzled, Jesse shook his head. "I don't know what you mean."

"The property is my gift to you if you will marry Gemma."

Jesse's hands curled into tight fists but he managed to keep his voice calm. "That is a surprising offer but I'm going to refuse."

Leroy lifted his hat and raked his fingers through his hair. "Gemma has given you a disgust of her. I feared as much."

Jesse scowled at the man he called a friend. "It is not Gemma I'm disgusted with, Leroy Lapp. Your daughter is worth far more than eighty acres of farmland. If you can't see that, then I pray *Gott* opens your eyes to the treasure you are so willing to cast aside. Does the love and respect of your child mean nothing to you? Or is it that the respect of others means more?"

Leroy stood staring at Jesse with his mouth open. Jesse spun on his heel and walked away before he said things he would regret, hoping Gemma never learned of this conversation.

Sunday came much too quickly for Gemma's liking. News of her condition and confession had spread. She knew by the way her mother had returned tight-lipped from her quilting circle and by the way her parents spoke in hushed tones when they thought she might be listening. From what she was able to gather, there was a disagreement in the community about how her case had been handled.

She arrived early at Bethany and Michael's home because she needed to keep busy. It had snowed again during the night, and the world sparkled under a fresh blanket of white. She worked in the kitchen getting pies cut and bread sliced as the families arrived one by one. Many of the people she knew greeted her openly and she began to relax. It wasn't until the new families arrived that she was ignored when they brought their baskets of food in before the meeting started. She saw the unease on her mother's face and wished she knew how to smooth things over.

Out the kitchen window, she watched the men unloading the bench wagon and carrying the backless wooden benches into the living room for when the service would be held. Jesse was among them. He was easy to pick out from the men dressed alike in dark pants, coats and hats. He stood a head taller than everyone. Just the sight of him brought her comfort. She would have a chance to spend some time with him after the meal had been served. She kept that thought at the forefront of her mind.

When the benches were set up on both sides of a center aisle, the women dried their hands and tidied their aprons before they filed in to take their places on one side of the room. Many of the men were already seated.

Gemma had to take her place among the unmarried women while her mother and her friends sat in the front rows. She was relieved when Jenny squeezed in beside her.

Jenny grasped Gemma's hand. "I'm so happy you are home. I missed you."

Gemma squeezed the girl's fingers. "I missed you too," she whispered.

Her father, Bishop Shultz and Samuel Yoder came into the room and hung their hats on pegs by the door. The three men had been discussing the preaching that would be done that morning. None of them had any formal training in the ministry. They had been chosen by lot to bring God's word to the congregation. It was a lifelong appointment without pay or benefits of any kind. They spoke from the heart without notes or prepared sermons. It was a responsibility every baptized Amish man agreed to accept should he be chosen.

The preaching lasted for three and a half hours. Each man took his turn reading passages from the German Bible and explaining what those words meant to the congregation. Their theme was about forgiveness and the prodigal son. Gemma couldn't help but feel they were speaking about her. She laid a hand over her stomach. She also had to forgive in order to find peace. She let go of her bitterness against Robert.

After the service was over, Gemma headed to the kitchen again to help serve the meal. Her friends were already getting things set up. No one needed directions. Everyone simply pitched in and began working. Gemma saw they were running low on clean glasses. She opened the cabinet door above her to pull out another stack when two women bringing in the dirty dishes walked past her.

"It's astounding that the minister's daughter didn't have to make a public confession."

"It certainly doesn't seem appropriate to me."

Gemma closed the cabinet door. There was a sharp intake of breath, but she didn't see which woman made the sound. Her eyes were pinned to the floor as her face grew hot with shame.

"Would you have forgiven her?" Bethany asked in a tight voice.

Gemma glanced up. A woman in her midfifties stood holding a stack of dirty plates. Behind her, a younger woman Gemma thought must be her daughter stood with her arms crossed over her chest.

"Of course," the older woman said. "After a suitable period of shunning. That is how the bishop from our previous congregation would have handled it."

"A suitable period?" Gemma heard the anger in Bethany's voice and cringed.

"Five or six weeks."

"Then I'm thankful our bishop has a more forgiving nature." They all turned to see Jesse filling the doorway with a fierce scowl on his face. The women gaped as he moved to stand beside Gemma. He slipped an arm around her shoulder. She wanted to sink into him and hide her face, but she willed herself to remain still.

"I heard how you claim to have been lost in the wilderness together. What a cozy story," the young woman said with sweet sarcasm. "Perhaps the babe is yours."

Gemma gasped, ready to refute the statement, but Jesse spoke first. "The child is not mine by blood but should Gemma agree to marry me, the babe will become *my son* or *my daughter* and will be cherished in my home and in my heart for all my life. Of that you can be certain."

Gemma was too stunned to speak.

Bethany took a step toward the women with a frozen smile on her face. "I will certainly mention your criticism of Bishop Shultz's decision to him. What was your last bishop's feelings about people who disparaged him behind his back?"

The two women turned on their heels and left the kitchen without another word, taking the dirty dishes with them. Gemma shook her head sadly. "Bethany, you shouldn't defend me."

"Accept it and rejoice. Besides, I was defending Bishop Schultz, not you."

"Who are they?" Jesse asked.

Gemma looked through the doorway into the living room, where the women were collecting their children.

"Newcomers. Agnes Martin and her daughter, Penelope." Bethany waved one hand. "Pay them no mind. If their last congregation was so wonderful, why did they move here? And now I am being judgmental and unkind. I will go apologize as soon as I'm finished cleaning up."

"I think they are leaving," Gemma told her, unable to look at Jesse yet. Why had he implied she might marry him?

Bethany smiled. "What a shame. My apology will have to wait, won't it?"

Jesse turned to Gemma. "I'm going to take the bench wagon to your father's place. He said your mother has a headache and he is taking her home. I told him I'd see that you got home too. Would you care to ride along with me? We have a lot to discuss."

"We do. *Danki*, Jesse. I will be out in a few minutes."

He nodded and walked away.

Bethany sank back against the counter. "If you don't marry that man, you are a bigger fool than I can imagine. The way he spoke of your baby becoming his— it almost melted my heart. I could hear how much he wants to be a father. I never would have guessed that about Jesse. He would be a good father and a fine husband to you."

"He is a man with many layers, but I'm not going to marry him." She put on her coat and went out to meet him.

Chapter Eleven

Jesse stood beside the wagon, waiting for Gemma to come out. What was she thinking? Had she been appalled by his confrontation with the two women? He was a bit ashamed of letting his temper out, but he didn't like watching somebody be bullied without speaking up. Especially Gemma.

The door opened, and she came out. He silently helped her into the wagon seat and climbed up beside her. He picked up the reins and headed the team toward Gemma's home. After several long minutes of silence, he couldn't stand it anymore. "I reckon I should explain myself."

"You don't need to."

He glanced at her. "Why do you say that?"

"Because you spoke to defend me, and I thank you for that. I know you weren't serious about marrying me."

"Can I ask you something?"

"Of course."

"Do you still think about him?"

"Who?"

"The father of your child."

"Robert? Actually, I haven't thought about him much at all this week except to realize I must forgive him."

Jesse smiled to himself. "That's a good thing." He clicked his tongue to get the horses moving faster. "Have you given any thought to my proposal?"

"Why should I?"

"What would you say if I told you I was serious?"

She frowned. "Is this some kind of joke?"

"Nope."

Her eyes widened. "Are you out of your mind?"

"You proposed to me once, and I'm saying yes now."

She shook her head as if to clear it. "That's ridiculous. You can't be serious, Jesse. Stop teasing. It isn't funny anymore."

He turned the team into the lane that led to her house and drew them to a stop by the front gate. He got down and helped her off the wagon. He stood with his hands resting lightly on her shoulders. "I am serious, Gemma. I wish to marry you."

"Why?"

He smiled at her bluntness. "I like you. You need a husband and your babe will need a father. I know you don't love me. That doesn't matter. We get along quite well. I'm offering you a marriage in name only."

"What about more children?"

"One is enough for me. My farm isn't large. I don't have much to offer now, but I will take care of you. You'll never be hungry in my house."

"I don't know what to say?"

"I believe yes and no are the most often used replies."

"I need to think about this."

"Of course."

Gemma walked before him into the house. Her par-

ents were in the living room. Gemma went and sat in
a chair in the corner of the room with her head down
and her hands clasped together in her lap. Her mother,
Dinah, watched Jesse closely.

He rubbed his suddenly damp hands on his pants.
What would her father think of his change of heart? It
wasn't because of the land. Jesse would have to make
sure Leroy understood that. He was doing it because
Gemma needed him. "Leroy, I wish to marry your
daughter. I am hoping you will see the benefits and
encourage her to accept me."

Gemma clutched her fingers together tightly. "Oh,
Jesse, don't do this."

Leroy stroked his beard. "You are a generous, hard-
working man. I could not ask for a better son-in-law,
but after what you said yesterday, you can see why I'm
surprised to hear this. Have you changed your mind?"

"I have not. Our conversation yesterday has nothing
to do with my decision today."

Gemma looked from one to the other. "What are the
two of you talking about? What conversation?"

Jesse smiled at her. "It's not important. What is important is your answer."

Her father stared hard at Jesse. "Why do you wish
to marry Gemma?"

"He is doing it because he feels sorry for me,"
Gemma said quickly. "I will be fine, Jesse. You don't
need to take care of me anymore."

Her father frowned at her. "I must ask you again,
Jesse. Why offer for my daughter's hand, knowing she
carries another man's child?"

"I've decided I'm ready to settle down. I've never

found a woman who suits me. I believe Gemma and I will get along well once the scandal blows over."

"He doesn't love me, *Daed*," Gemma interjected. She fell silent beneath her father's glare.

"Love grows from respect," he said before turning back to Jesse.

Jesse's chance to wed Gemma did not hinge on what her father had to say. She had a choice. He didn't want her to feel pressured into marrying him. He wanted her to agree that this was best for her and the baby.

Her father turned to her mother. "*Mudder*, what is your feeling about this?"

"If she marries Jesse, I will see my grandchild as often as I want, but that is not a reason to wed. You must believe that God has chosen you for each other."

"That's why I can't marry you, Jesse. He didn't choose us for each other."

"I disagree. May I speak with Gemma in private?" Jesse looked from her mother to her father.

Her father nodded and beckoned to his wife. "Listen closely to him, Gemma. Jesse has a *goot* head on his shoulders. You have brought shame to this family. Your mother and I forgive you, but what you decide will ultimately affect us too. Do you understand that?"

She nodded.

Her parents left the room together. She held her hands wide. "I know you don't love me."

He pulled another chair over until he sat in front of her. He took her hands in his. "Love isn't necessary to have a good marriage. I care about you, Gemma. We are friends, remember? Why did God put us together in the wilderness if not to learn about each other and grow in our affections? You care about me, I know you do."

"And that's why I can see that you are making a mistake. There will still be talk. People will know you aren't the father."

"That's true, but the talk will die down in time and people will forget."

"Maybe they will, but can you forget he or she isn't your flesh and blood? Can you expect me to forget that?"

"In time, I hope we both look at the babe and see only the child of our hearts."

"I don't love you."

He flinched at the pain of her words. "I know, but we like each other, right? I won't expect what you can't give me. It will be a marriage in name only for the sake of your baby. Our baby."

She stood up suddenly. "I need some time. I can't make a decision today."

She rushed past Jesse and up the stairs, limping heavily. He heard her bedroom door slam.

Leroy and Dinah came back into the living room. "Well?" Leroy asked. He looked worn down and sad as did Dinah. Gemma's condition had inflicted a toll on her parents. Their disappointment had to be deep and soul shaking.

"She wants some time to think it over."

Her mother stared into Jesse's eyes. "I believe she will make the right decision. She is our only child and perhaps we have spoiled her because of that, but she has a good heart. If she rejects you at first, be prepared to be patient with her. Can you do that?"

He glanced up the stairs. "*Ja*, I can be patient. Tell her to come see me when she has an answer."

"My offer of the property still stands if she agrees," Leroy said.

His wife scowled at him. "I can't believe how foolish you are. Can't you see Jesse has her best interest at heart and not his own?"

Jesse smiled at her and nodded. "My answer is still the same. Keep your land. I will only wed Gemma if she wants to."

Gemma threw herself down on her bed and clutched the quilt tightly in each hand. She knew why Jesse had offered for her. He was still trying to protect her the way he had in the wilderness. It was noble, but she couldn't accept such a sacrifice from him. She wanted to keep the friendship they had found while they were snow-bound in the cabin.

She turned over to stare at the ceiling. Would marriage allow them to remain friends, or would it change everything? It was easy to imagine spending her days keeping house for him, fixing his meals and helping him farm, but there was more to marriage than that. Didn't he deserve the chance to marry for love and be happy with a wife who loved him in return? If she wedded him, she was robbing him of that chance. She wouldn't hurt him in the long run because he was determined to help her now. She cared too much to allow that to happen.

The next morning, she made her way downstairs. It was late. To her surprise, her father was still sitting at the kitchen table. She poured herself a cup of coffee and sat down, expecting more of his silent treatment.

"How are you feeling?"

She looked up in surprise. "Not bad."

"Your mother had the worst morning sickness when she was pregnant with you. It went on for weeks."

A wry smile curved her lips. "Is that where I got it from?"

"Not from me. I'm never sick."

They both fell silent for a while. He cleared his throat and she expected him to speak but he didn't.

"How is Mother's headache?" Gemma asked to break the silence.

"Better once she didn't have to listen to the bishop's wife go on and on about her new grandbaby."

Gemma looked down. "I don't know what else I can say except I'm sorry."

"I too am sorry. I've been hard on you out of false pride. I hope you can forgive me."

"There's nothing to forgive." She managed a slight smile for him.

"Have you given thought to Jesse's proposal?"

"Only all night long. I'm going to see him now."

"What are you going to tell him?"

"I hope I'll have the right answer when I see him."

Jesse didn't think anything about Leroy's buggy turning into the shed building site. It wasn't until he heard someone cough that he stopped hammering and turned to see who it was. Gemma sat in the buggy with her hands clasped in front of her. She wore her gray cloak and her black traveling bonnet. "*Guder mariye*, Jesse."

"Good morning to you, Gemma. Have you come to any decision?" He held his breath, not knowing if he was pushing her too hard.

"I like you a lot, Jesse. I believe you will make a good father. But there is more to a marriage than that."

"I would try my best." He walked to the buggy.

She didn't get out. "Does it bother you that there would only be friendship between us, not love?"

It shouldn't have bothered him. Love wasn't something he claimed to want or need, so why did the lack of it trouble him? He shook off the foolish thought. "Love isn't necessary to start a marriage. Affection can grow over time. So can respect and compassion. These are things that make a strong marriage."

Was he convincing her? He pulled the buggy door open to help her down.

She braced her hands on his shoulders as he swung her off the seat and deposited her in front of him. He kept his hands on her waist. "I'm still waiting for an answer."

"I'm not trying to string you along. I have to make the right decision for me and for my child."

"I couldn't agree with you more. I'm a patient man." He leaned close to her ear. "Do I stand a chance?"

She tried not to smile but lost the battle. "A small one."

He could feel her wavering. "Give me that chance and I'll make a good life for you and your babe, I promise. I know I can make you happy, Gemma. We can build a good life here close to your family and the friends you love. Your mother will have her grandchild close by. Your little one will have Anna's and Bethany's children as playmates. We can even travel to Florida for a vacation once in a while. Please say you'll marry me."

Jesse had given her every reason to say yes, except the one she wanted to hear. That he loved her. She knew he didn't. She was foolish to think he might. Hadn't she learned her lesson yet?

If she said yes, it would be for the baby's sake and not because she was head over heels in love with Jesse. Love couldn't be trusted. Her baby would have a home, and she would have her family and friends near. She would have Jesse's companionship for the rest of her days.

"I'm giving you a chance to back out right now, Jesse Crump. You can live your life as a free man without any unwelcome burdens."

The corner of his mouth lifted in a slow grin that spread across his face as his eyes sparkled. "Sounds dull, don't you think? Who will I find to gather bark with me?"

She couldn't resist his smile. "You win, Jesse Crump. I will marry you."

"You will?"

"I will."

He wrapped his arms around her and pulled her close. Her cheek rested against his chest as he tucked her beneath his chin. "You won't regret this. I vow it."

She expected the hug but she hadn't expected it would feel so sweet or that she would want more.

The bishop came out carrying a sheet of plywood. "Jesse. Gemma, nice to see you."

Gemma glanced sheepishly at Jesse. "I've come to tell you I have accepted Jesse's proposal."

"That's *wunderbar*. Have you chosen a date?"

Gemma glanced at Jesse. He shrugged.

She turned back to the bishop. "I'll have to see what my parents want to do."

"Meet with me again when you have a day." He tipped his hat and walked on.

Jesse helped her back into the buggy. He held her hand a few moments longer than necessary. "I'll see you soon." He started to walk away.

"Jesse?"

He turned back to her. "What?"

"I promise to try to be the best possible wife." She meant it.

"And I promise to try to be the best possible husband."

Thirty minutes later, Gemma found her mother lying down with a cold compress on her forehead in her darkened bedroom.

"Oh, *Mamm*, do you have another headache? Can I get you something?"

Her mother held out her hand. "That's sweet, but I'm okay. What do you need?"

"I came to tell you that I've decided to accept Jesse's offer."

Mamm sat up. "You have?"

Gemma nodded and clasped her hands together.

"It won't be a big wedding since it will be rushed, but I want a nice one for you. Does Jesse have much family?" *Mamm* asked.

"Only his mother as far as I know."

"I can have everything ready in three weeks' time. Have you set a date?"

Gemma was pleased to see her mother so animated. "Not yet. We will want to visit with the bishop before we make any firm plans."

"Yes, of course. We'll need to start on your wedding dress right away. And we will need to pick out invitations and make a guest list. I hope that is enough time for your cousins in Pennsylvania to get here. We'll have to get those in the mail first. I need to make a list." She tossed back the quilt and got out of bed.

She embraced Gemma. "I have dreamed of your wedding for a long time. Bless you. I want you to be happy."

"I don't need a big wedding," Gemma said. She had caused so much grief for her parents. She had to hope this was the way to repair it. She would never cause her family such pain again.

Her mother patted Gemma's cheek. "The wedding won't be big, but it should be a happy day to remember all your life. Leave it to me."

Several days later Jesse drove briskly along the road that led past his house. Gemma sat beside him in the buggy. He was worried about what she would think of his home. It would be hers too. He hoped she would like the farm as much as he did. Since his proposal, she had been quiet and subdued, unlike the Gemma he knew, and he wasn't sure how to bring back his friend.

Bachelor, recluse, dog lover, Jesse was afraid his home showed the main aspects of his life clearly. He had intended to give the place a makeover before bringing a woman home, but there wasn't much time before the coming wedding. It was the custom for newlyweds to live with the bride's parents for several months or even a year after the wedding. He didn't want to wait that long.

He stopped by the gate, opened the buggy door and offered Gemma his hand. He prayed he wasn't about to make things worse between them. "This is my farm.

Sixty acres. House, barn, chicken house, four outbuildings and a pretty view."

He was relieved to see a spark of enthusiasm come into her eyes. She placed her hand in his. "I'm glad you brought me here."

"I wanted you to see what you were getting into. It's not as fine as your father's house, but it's home."

"Will I be able to make changes? Oh, I didn't mean that as a criticism." She dropped her voice and her gaze.

He leaned close. "Gemma, I like a person who isn't afraid to tell me what they think."

She raised her eyes to meet his gaze. "Are you sure you do?"

"Of course. I like you, and you've given me a piece of your mind plenty of times."

She cracked a tiny smile. "Only when you needed it," she said sweetly.

"Needed it? Ha." He waved a hand toward the two-story farmhouse in need of a coat of paint, with mismatched shingles on the roof and overgrown trees sprouting along the foundation. His team of Belgian geldings stood in a corral by the barn, watching the activity with interest. He noticed the fence could use a coat of paint too. He had been letting the place go. "This is my humble home. Our home."

"It's nice," she said.

"That is not an honest opinion."

She gave him a cheeky grin. "Okay. It needs work, but it has wonderful potential."

He chuckled. "I would have stopped at *it needs work*. I haven't had much time or money to fix it up. I've been putting money aside for more land." He pushed away the thought that he could have gained what he wanted by accepting her father's offer. Gemma was here because she wanted to be, not because her father wanted her off his hands. She was here because Jesse wanted her to be a part of his life too.

Jesse opened the front door for his bride-to-be. He was tickled to see the sassy woman with witty comebacks starting to reemerge from the worried, subdued woman she had become in her father's house.

Gemma paused at the door of his home. She leaned forward and peeked in. "Is it safe?"

He shook his head as he placed a hand on her lower back and guided her through the door. "Depends on where you stand."

Her gaze went to the far wall, where the ceiling was marred by a large water stain that had made the plaster sag. A tiny frown creased her forehead. She slowly scanned the room, taking in the long worn-looking wooden table that had been handed down from his grandparents. It was stacked with groceries he hadn't taken the time to put away. She studied the fireplace and then the stove. Both needed a good cleaning. The corners of her mouth pulled downward. At the sight of Roscoe's food and water dishes by the table, her lips curled inward. She pressed them together hard.

"Are you pleased?"

She opened her mouth as if to speak, closed it and opened it again. "*Ja.* Of course."

Then she clasped her hands in front of her. He noticed she rubbed and twisted her intertwined fingers. He grinned. She wanted to say something else. There was a glint in her eyes. The woman he knew before she went away to Florida would never have held back her opinion in this manner. The words would have popped out before she had even thought through her comment.

And I would have grumbled at her for it. I was a fool. I reckon both of us have changed.

"Let me show you around. A woman should know her way around the house she is to keep. Don't you agree?"

She nodded, but before they could start the tour, Roscoe bolted in, knocking Gemma off balance. Instinctively, Jesse braced her.

"Oh," she gasped as she clung to him.

Roscoe sat facing them by the edge of the table, his bowl at his feet. He woofed once.

"No scraps yet, boy." Jesse moved away from Gemma to scratch the dog's head.

"He eats in here?" Her voice showed her disapproval.

"Of course." He hid a grin. She was going to learn that she could disagree with him without being chastised.

The Gemma he wanted to see, the one who aggravated him to the point of distraction, wouldn't allow a farm dog to eat in her kitchen. A smile grew in his heart. He hoped this tour would coax her out of her shell and get them back to the friendship they had enjoyed in the cabin.

"He sits at the table with me most nights. Just like a person. Don't worry. I don't think he'll mind having you join us."

Gemma approached the table and ran her hand along the back of the two chairs. "Join you?" She clasped her hands together again. "Does that mean we'll need to add another chair?" That was not what she wanted to ask or how she wanted to ask it. He could tell by the twitch in her jaw.

"I suppose so." He motioned toward Roscoe. "Go lie down." He held his breath.

Roscoe trotted to the bedroom. Gemma frowned as she examined the bare kitchen.

"What do you think? It needs a woman's touch, but you can give it a go if you want."

"Some curtains would be lovely."

"Curtains? I'm not sure that's necessary. Plain shades do well enough. Roscoe might pull them down." He folded his arms tight across his chest to keep from laughing at her expression.

"We'll have to get some china for that cabinet." She brightened as she gestured to the large empty china hutch nestled in a nook behind the dining table.

"China? I have these. Can't break them." He picked up a plastic dish, of which he owned only enough for him and Roscoe.

"But…" She started to say something, but hesitated.

"You wouldn't be able to reach all the shelves anyway, short stuff." He placed the dish on the top ledge. "Try."

Her eyes flashed in his direction. "Are you trying to pick a fight? Because if you are, you are about to get one."

He cocked one eyebrow. "No, dear."

"Don't *dear* me." She scooted past him into the living room and stopped short at the old worn-down couch under the window. Then she turned and looked in the other rooms.

When he'd moved to New Covenant, he hadn't thought of outfitting a home for a family. Any money he had went back into the farm. There was enough furniture for one man. That was all. He watched her face contort as she noticed the sparseness of the home. When she reached the first bedroom doorway, she let out a small shriek. He stepped up behind her and peered in to see Roscoe curled in the middle of the quilt on his bed.

"Good boy."

"Good boy?" Gemma asked in disbelief.

"He's lying down. He did as I told him. He'll get over and share the space with you when you're ready for bed."

"Is this where he usually sleeps? Because I'm not sleeping with a dog. Where is my room?" Her voice was rising. He smothered a grin.

"The next door down the hall. Where else would Roscoe sleep if not in your or my bed?"

"Outside! That's where animals sleep. And eat, for that matter. His job is to guard the farm. I don't want a dog slobbering where I'll be feeding the baby."

"That's not right. There's no bed for him out there."

"Actually, there's no bed for him in here. That is a bed for people, not dogs. I'm sure there is a perfectly good napping spot for him outdoors." That determined, bossy tone inched its way back into her voice.

He kept prodding. "It doesn't seem fair to make him sleep and eat outside."

She cocked her head and blinked. He turned away to keep from laughing. "Speaking of meals, I do expect breakfast at sunrise. Freshly baked bread, eggs and bacon will do. Roscoe prefers his eggs scrambled. I like mine over hard. How are you at housework?"

Jesse grabbed the broom that was standing in the

corner. "I guess we will find out. We'll have your first lesson now." He pushed the broom toward her.

She crossed her arms and arched one eyebrow. "You intend to teach me how to use a broom? Are you serious?"

"We could start with the dusting, if you wish."

Her mouth dropped open.

"Or the cooking. There are several delicious ways to serve white pine bark and cattail roots."

The way her eyes narrowed told him she was finally onto him. A smile tugged at her lips and then blossomed into a grin. Her eyes sparkled. She jerked the broom from his grasp and beat at his boots until she backed him out the kitchen door onto the porch.

"Jesse Crump. I know how to cook a decent meal without boiling tree bark. I will sew curtains for the kitchen. Roscoe can eat his meals and take his naps on the porch, and if I can't reach the top shelf of the china cabinet, I will use a stepladder to retrieve my china myself."

He propped his hands on his hips and tipped his head. "Stepladder? What's that? I don't believe I've ever had the need for one of those before." He stepped up beside her and placed one palm against the porch ceiling.

"Show-off."

He gave a hoot of laughter.

"You're making fun of me." She turned her face away in mock anger.

"I'm not. I like a woman who knows how to laugh. You do that so well."

She raised the broom as if to swat him like an annoying giant housefly. He caught it and pulled her toward him. He leaned in until their faces were inches apart.

"I know it's not a cabin in the woods, but we can

joke, laugh, tease each other, even argue within these walls and never worry about losing our friendship. Agreed?"

She laid a hand on his cheek. "Agreed."

"Welcome home, Gemma."

"I like the sound of that."

He gazed into her lively eyes and realized he was starting to fall for his bride-to-be. He was going to do everything within his power to see that she had a comfortable life and never regretted their marriage.

Was there a remote chance that she could someday care for him as more than a friend? If not, had he signed on for a lifetime of hiding his pain? It was wisest to remain her friend and never hope for more.

On Wednesday morning, Gemma and her mother were preparing to go into the city to start shopping for the wedding. Gemma had an OB-GYN doctor's appointment at ten o'clock that had been made by the emergency room nurse in Cleary. The day was snowy and gray, and it suited Gemma's mood. The doctor's visit was a reminder that her baby's life was always in danger.

Her mother's mare had already been harnessed to the buggy and she stood patiently waiting at the gate. The two women started out the door and met Jesse. He tipped his hat. "Leroy has asked me to drive you. I am ready when you are."

"That's very kind of you. I have a lot of errands today, and Gemma is to see the doctor."

He turned a look of concern on Gemma. "Are you ill? Is something wrong?"

She shook her head and replied meekly, "It is a simple pregnancy checkup. I'm fine."

"I would like to hear what the doctor has to say, if you don't mind."

"That is a *goot* idea," *Mamm* said as she climbed into the back of the buggy. "You can get your marriage license today too."

"Don't we have to get blood drawn or something before we get married?" Jesse asked.

"Not in Maine," Gemma said. "I already asked Bethany about it."

It took almost an hour to reach the outskirts of Presque Isle. Fortunately, the traffic wasn't heavy. They visited the fabric store first and chose a periwinkle blue material for Gemma's wedding dress. After that, they found a printer that could do an order of a hundred invitations that same day. They would need to get them in the mail tomorrow in order to give family members in Pennsylvania and the neighboring Maine Amish communities enough notice to attend. Weddings were the most common way that Amish young people from different districts met each other and for far-flung relatives to reconnect.

They arrived at the obstetrician's office a few minutes before ten o'clock. Gemma filled out the paperwork required and waited nervously to see the doctor.

Dr. Thomas turned out to be a young woman with short dark curly hair who immediately put Gemma at ease. Following the examination, she had Gemma's mother and Jesse step into the room. "I'm pleased to meet all of you. I want to congratulate you on your new family-member-to-be. As the doctor in Cleary told you, Gemma, there is a problem with your pregnancy. In your case, you have what is called a partial placenta previa."

Gemma tried to absorb all the information the doctor

gave her. She stressed the need for limited travel and bed rest as much as possible. It would mean a cesarean birth. Any labor could cause bleeding and jeopardize the life of both the mother and the baby.

"I understand you have a midwife in your community. She can manage you at home, but you will have to come here for the delivery. You are already twenty-six weeks along, and that is good. The goal is to get you as close to full term as possible and deliver you safely by C-section. I'm going to send some instructions home with you. It's important that you follow them. I'm also going to give you a steroid injection that will help mature your baby's lungs if it is born prematurely. Do you have any questions?"

After they left the office and reached their buggy, Jesse took Gemma's elbow to help her in. "That was a lot to take in. How are you?"

"I'm fine." It was a lie. She was terrified. She could lose her baby. The baby she hadn't wanted but had grown to love in spite of everything.

"I'm scared," he admitted.

Gemma nodded. "I am too."

Her mother took Gemma's hands between her own. "Our faith is in the Lord. In Isaiah 41:10, he tells us, 'Fear thou not; for I am with thee: be not dismayed; for I am thy God: I will strengthen thee; yea, I will help thee; yea, I will uphold thee with the right hand of my righteousness.'"

"I believe in the goodness of the Lord," Gemma said, struggling to find the faith beneath her words, but a deep sense of foreboding wouldn't leave her in peace.

Chapter Twelve

Gemma discovered that her family and friends had taken her doctor's instructions to heart. She wasn't allowed to lift a finger if anyone was around to watch her. Anytime she tried to do something for herself, she was scolded by her mother as if she were still an unruly toddler.

A week after her visit to the doctor, Gemma met the midwife, Esther Hopper. Esther was a jovial plump woman in her late fifties with short gray hair, who claimed her greatest joy in life was delivering babies.

Gemma was curled up on the sofa with a blanket over her lap, at her mother's insistence, when Esther breezed into the room. "Finally, I have a patient I don't have to track down."

Bethany and Anna followed the woman in bright pink scrubs beneath a red plaid coat into the room and took their places on each side of Gemma. Esther glanced at the group. "I believe I will just hold clinic here each time I need to see you ladies."

"What exactly is wrong with Gemma?" Anna asked.

"She has tried explaining it to us, but we really don't understand."

"Gemma, may I discuss your case with your friends? I can't give them any information unless you allow me to. HIPAA and all that jazz. That would be the government regulations regarding patient privacy."

Gemma folded her arms across her chest. "I want them to know that I do not have to be chained to a bed or the sofa."

"Unfortunately, that is about the size of it. It is important that you don't do anything strenuous. I'm going to leave a cell phone with you, Gemma. I have your bishop's permission for you to use it in an emergency. I consider an emergency anytime you need to talk to me or anytime you have a question. My number is the first one. The only other number you should know is 911. At the first sign of labor, even if you are not sure it is labor, that is the number I want you to call. Understood?"

"Understood," all three of them said together and giggled.

Esther smiled. "You are blessed, Gemma, to have a support group at your fingertips. I'm sure you and your baby are going to be just fine."

After explaining Gemma's condition and using a nursing textbook illustration to help the women understand, she completed her paperwork and her exam of Gemma and pronounced her in excellent health. She brought out a small white boxlike machine from her bag. "This is a Doppler. It will allow the mother to hear the baby's heartbeat."

There was a knock at the door. Anna went to answer it. She came back into the room. "It's Jesse. May he come in?"

Gemma nodded. A few seconds later, he came in with his hat in hand. Esther introduced herself and said, "You are just in time." She positioned a wand on Gemma's tummy and immediately the *thud-thud-thud* of the baby's heartbeat filled the room. Gemma listened in awe.

"Is that her?" Jesse's voice cracked with emotion.

"Well, it might be a him, but yes, this is your baby's heartbeat. Amazing, isn't it? Every time I hear one I think how...amazing."

After Esther packed up her stuff and promised to return in two weeks, Bethany and Anna left with her. Jesse remained. He sat down beside Gemma. "How are you today? Don't say fine."

She kept her eyes downcast. The wedding was fast approaching, yet it didn't feel real. It would be a wedding without a courtship or a wedding trip because she would still be on bed rest in her mother's house until her babe was born. It was also going to be a wedding without love. Maybe it would be better to call off the ceremony until after the birth. She glanced at Jesse to tell him that and couldn't find the words. "I finished all the invitations."

"That's *goot*."

"I wanted to ask if you... Would you like me to send one to your mother? I don't have her address."

"Of course."

She handed him an envelope and he scrawled his mother's name and address across it. "I doubt she will come, but you never know." He handed it back.

"How have you been?" she asked.

"Busy. We have a lot of new orders. The bishop is thinking about hiring another man."

"It's wonderful that his business is doing well." She smoothed her hand over the blanket on her lap. He grasped her hand and held it gently.

"Gemma, is there something wrong?" Jesse asked. Her hand remained limp in his.

She didn't look at him. "*Mamm* has the wedding plans well in hand. The baby and I are doing okay."

"You seem distant."

"I'm right here." She pulled away from him.

"That's not what I meant."

She finally looked up. "You are worrying about nothing. I'm fine. I think I would like to take a nap now."

"Okay. I'll see you again tomorrow." He leaned over and kissed her cheek.

Her eyes filled with tears at the unexpected gesture. He took her hand again. "Tell me what's wrong. You can trust me. We are friends, remember?"

"What if I lose this baby? I listen to the doctor and the midwife and I'm afraid. What if we marry and then lose my child? Then you will be bound to me for no reason."

He adjusted the blanket over her shoulders. "We can't see the road ahead. We have to trust that we are walking the path meant for us. If the worst should happen— we will endure it. I will be bound to you because that is my choice."

"I'm just tired. Please go."

He didn't want to leave but had little choice. He left the Lapp farm and drove his buggy to Michael's place. Michael had a workshop attached to the house. Jesse entered through the side door. Inside the shop, the walls were covered with clocks in various stages of repair.

A workbench sat in front of the large window. A half a dozen pocket watches sitting in padded boxes, a large magnifying glass and a jeweler's loupe were neatly arranged on it.

Across the room, Michael's dog, Sadie, lay curled on a rag rug in a patch of sunshine. Sadie got up and came to greet Jesse with her tail wagging. He scratched her behind her ears and patted her head. Satisfied with that much attention, she went back to her rug. No one else was around. Jesse was on the point of leaving when the door opened and Michael's brother-in-law, Ivan, walked in. He was intent on studying a beautifully etched gold pocket watch. He looked up and grinned. "Hey, Jesse, didn't see you there."

Jesse chuckled. "I don't hear that very often."

"I imagine not. What brings you here?"

"I wanted to speak to Michael."

Ivan put down the watch and turned his stool to face Jesse. "I heard you are getting married. Congratulations. I have to say, it came as a big shock to me."

"To me too. Sort of." Jesse sat down and leaned back against the workbench. He was always afraid of breaking something inside Michael's shop. He didn't see how his friend could enjoy working with things that were so small he needed a magnifying glass to put them together.

"Want to tell me about it?" Ivan asked.

"Actually, I was hoping for some advice from Michael."

"If you want advice about clocks, ask Michael. If you want advice about girls, I'm your man."

"How old are you?"

Ivan puffed up his chest, slipped his thumbs under

his suspenders and stretched them out. "Almost sixteen, and the ladies love me."

"If I want advice on being a braggart, I'll know who to see."

Ivan chuckled. "I thought it sounded pretty good. I over did it, huh?"

"By quite a bit. Where's Michael?" Jesse asked.

"In the kitchen. I'll go get him."

After Ivan left, Jesse leaned forward and propped his elbows on his knees. He wasn't sure how much of the situation to share with Michael, but he needed help. When his friend came in, Jesse sat up straight. "Your brother-in-law is getting too big for his britches."

"You aren't telling me anything new. What's up?"

"I need some advice about Gemma. The closer the date of the wedding comes, the more remote Gemma seems."

Michael folded his arms over his chest. "You think she is getting cold feet? Marriage is forever. A lot of couples have second thoughts and doubts. You two must have them doubly so."

"Did you? Did Bethany?"

"I will admit to being nervous, but I never doubted that Bethany was the one for me. We were and still are very much in love. I don't know how it's possible to be much happier. Tell me something. Are you sure you don't love Gemma?"

Jesse rubbed his damp palms on his pant legs. His friend knew the reason he was getting married. "I care about her. She's cute and funny and her eyes light up when she sees me. She drives me crazy and makes me smile. I don't know if that is love, but I do know she needs someone to look after her and the baby. She is troubled, but she won't tell me about it. I thought you could ask Bethany to find out what Gemma is really thinking. If she is ready to call it off, I'll understand."

"Gemma, do you want to call off the wedding?"

Gemma was lying in bed in her room on the second floor of her mother's house. She glanced sharply at Bethany, who was sitting on a chair beside the bed. "Why would you ask such a thing?"

"Because Jesse asked Michael, who asked me to ask you if you want to call this thing off."

"Does Jesse want to?" Gemma's heart fell as she considered what that would mean. The marriage bans were to be read at the next church service.

Did it mean Jesse had changed his mind?

She looked at Bethany. "What if this is the wrong thing to do? Suppose he falls in love with someone after we are married. He'll resent me for denying him the chance at true love."

Bethany shook her head. "Not the Jesse I know. He doesn't hold a grudge. The same thing can face any couple. It is respect for God's law and respect for their partner that keeps them from acting on an attraction to someone else."

Gemma struggled to find something else wrong with marrying Jesse. "He's too big and tall. He makes me feel like a gnat beside him."

Bethany laughed out loud. "That is the lamest excuse I've ever heard for not marrying someone. I think you like Jesse Crump more than you're telling me and more than you'll admit to yourself."

Did she? The truthful answer was, yes, she did. She liked him a lot. Not in the same way as last year. That had been a girlish crush tied up with wishful thinking as much as anything. This was something deeper. Something real. And it changed things.

The more she grew to care about him, the more determined she became to avoid hurting him.

Bethany put her hands on her hips. "Are you asking me to ask Michael to ask Jesse if that's what he wants to do?"

"*Nee*, Jesse should be here after he gets off work today. I will ask him myself."

"That is the right answer. Is there anything else I can do for you?"

"*Nee*, I'm whining. I have vowed to do better, and already I am slipping."

"I would be out of my mind by now. I don't know how you can stay so calm."

"Because I must."

Bethany got up. "I'll be back tomorrow after church. Jenny and Ivan say hi."

"Bring them with you. I'd love to see them."

"They are excited about the wedding."

"I want all my friends in my wedding party. If there is going to be a wedding." Had Jesse really changed his mind? She chewed on her lower lip. A sharp pain ripped across her abdomen and she doubled over, clutching the covers to keep from crying out.

Bethany was at her side immediately. "What's wrong? Is it labor? Where is the phone?"

Gemma drew several quick breaths as the pain receded. "It's gone."

"Are you sure?"

"I think so. The phone is in the top drawer of my nightstand."

Bethany pulled it out and placed it in Gemma's hand. "Just in case."

Gemma's eyes filled with tears. "If I lose this baby, I don't know what I will do."

Bethany dropped to the bed and put her arms around Gemma. "You will do what women have done since the dawn of time. Keep on living. Have more children if God blesses you with them and know your babe is waiting for you in heaven."

"I didn't want it when I first found out. I wanted it to go away so I wouldn't be shamed."

"Which only proves that you are human. You want your babe now. You love your child, and he or she knows that."

"I hope so. I really hope so."

"I have to leave, but I'm going to get your mother to sit with you."

"She has so much to do already. I'm fine."

"Your *mamm* would forbid me to come again if I didn't tell her when her daughter needs her."

Bethany left, and a few minutes later Dinah marched into the room and up to Gemma's bedside. "It's the not knowing that's the worst, isn't it?"

Gemma nodded as tears slipped down her cheeks. Her mother gathered her in her arms and rocked her back and forth. "This is a hard time for you, I know. We have no way to see the future, so we fear what it holds. We make bargains with God. Save this child and I will give all my money to the needy. It's all right. Our Father understands our fears and our failings. He loves us just the same. We must humble ourselves before Him and pray that His will be done."

"What if I don't deserve this child?"

Her mother drew back. "What if you do?"

"I'm scared I won't be a good mother."

"We all are when that tiny naked thing is handed to us without a single set of instructions. And yet the world is full of grown people who walk and talk, so mothers do okay. *Liebchen*, I have more bad news."

"What now?"

"We don't have enough celery."

Gemma choked and then began laughing. "Oh, the horror of it. An Amish wedding without enough stewed celery to feed the guests. We'll be talked about behind our backs for years."

Jesse found Dinah and Gemma sitting beside each other on the bed, chuckling between sobs. They both had puffy red eyes. Fear hit him between the shoulder blades. "Is everything okay?"

"We don't have enough celery for the wedding dinner," Dinah said, getting up and walking out of the room.

"That is what you are crying about?"

Gemma wiped her face with her hands. "It's a disaster."

He sat down in the chair beside Gemma's bed. "I can arrange for a delivery of more celery."

She folded her hands on the quilt. "Do you want to call off the wedding?"

He tipped his head slightly, trying to read her face. "Do you?"

"I asked you first."

"Fair enough. I don't."

"Okay. Order more celery."

"That's it?"

"I can't think of anything else. Check with *Mamm*."

"Are we still okay?" he asked, not knowing what to expect.

"Are we still friends? We are, Jesse. We are."

Relief made him smile. "I'm glad, really glad. Someone asked me if we wanted a crib for the baby. Do you have one you want to use, or should I say yes?"

The light faded in her eyes. She traced the edge of the blocks on her quilt with one finger. "Let's wait on the baby things until—until after the wedding."

Chapter Thirteen

As was the custom among the Amish, Gemma and Jesse didn't attend the church service the day their intention to marry was announced. It was meant to give the engaged couple a day of rest before the rush of the final days leading up to the wedding, but Gemma had already had all the rest she could tolerate. She had convinced Esther to let her be up for a few hours while she cooked a meal for Jesse. Another Amish tradition. After that, she would go straight back to bed. Esther was going to stop in just to make sure she was following orders.

Gemma surveyed the food in the refrigerator. It was packed top to bottom with plastic containers, waiting to be served on Thursday. "What would you like to eat today?"

Jesse sat at the table, turning his fork around and around. "Doesn't matter."

He had retreated into his one- and two-word answers that made it impossible for her to tell what he was thinking. How had the wonderful bond they once shared vanished so completely?

"At least he didn't ask for pine bark," she muttered.

"What?" He looked her way.

"Nothing. Meatballs with rice sound okay?"

"Sure."

She measured out a pound of hamburger and formed it into balls, prepared the rice and some sliced vegetables, arranged the meatballs on top of the rice in a casserole dish and popped it into the oven to bake. After washing her hands, she set the kitchen timer and joined Jesse at the table.

"This is so nice." She sighed heavily and sat down.

"Spending the day with me, just the two of us?"

"That and cooking again. Standing at the sink. A hundred things I never thought I would miss until I couldn't do them."

The silence that followed proved she had missed a chance to connect with Jesse. She should not have lumped his company in with the kitchen chores.

"Have you heard from your mother?" she asked.

"Nothing."

"Did Dale get his truck fixed?"

"Yup."

She tapped her fingers on the tabletop. "More coffee?"

"Sure, but I can get it." He went to the stove and poured himself another cup.

He sat down with it but merely stared into the dark liquid. After a few minutes of silence, he looked at her. "Have you thought about names for the baby?"

She popped up and began searching in one of the cupboards. "I know I saw raisins."

She didn't want to pick a name to go on a headstone if the worst happened. She felt a twinge in her side. It subsided as quickly as it came on, but it was a pointed reminder of what could go wrong. She located the box she had been searching for. "Do you like raisins in your fruit salad?"

"Not really."

"Oh. Okay." She put the box back and returned to the table. Bracing her hands on her hips, she stretched her lower back.

"Are you hurting?"

In so many ways, Jesse. You have no idea.

She had spoken of her fear to him once. If she broadcast her concerns, they might come true. She didn't want Jesse to think she was whining about her condition. She would bear her fear in silence and humility. "I think I'll go and lie down. Call me when the timer goes off."

Gemma's next ten days were filled with watching everyone else make the final preparations for her big day. Hemming her wedding dress was all she was allowed to do. She'd chosen a deep blue material called Persian blue for her outfit and hoped that Jesse would approve. She was lying in bed or on the sofa as her friends helped her mother bake and clean the house. Jesse came by every day, but they seemed to have less and less to say to each other.

The day before the wedding, her married friends and members of the church arrived to prepare for the dinner. A meal would be served after the ceremony, but the celebration would continue long into the evening. A second meal would be needed for the guests who remained. When one of her mother's helpers didn't show up, Gemma was allowed back in the kitchen for a short time to wash dishes and ice the cake.

By the time the house settled in that evening, she

was dead tired and her feet were swollen. Although her sprain had healed, it still ached when she was up on her feet too much. Like now. She lit the lamp in her room and stared at the worn-out-looking woman staring back at her in the bedroom mirror. She stuck her tongue out at her reflection. "So much for a beautiful bride. I hope Jesse doesn't mind settling for a haggard-looking one."

Something rattled against her window. A few seconds later, the sound came again. What was going on? She went to the window and looked down. Jesse was searching for something at his feet. She raised the window and leaned out. "What are you doing?"

"Trying to see my fiancée. Come down."

As tired as she was, she still wanted to spend time with him. But why was he here? Had he come to tell her he had changed his mind? She wouldn't blame him if he had. She went downstairs and opened the back door. She held a finger to her lips as she slipped out beside him. "My *aenti* and cousins are sleeping on cots just inside. What do you want?"

He grasped both her hands in his. "An uninterrupted moment with my wife-to-be. Is that too much to ask?"

"I thought perhaps you had come to call it off."

"I promised I would take care of you, Gemma. I won't go back on that promise. Not now and not ever." He squeezed her fingers.

She was trusting him with her future and the future of her child. He was an honorable man and he would keep his word. "You deserve better than you are getting, Jesse Crump."

"I think the opposite is true. Want to go for a buggy ride? We won't really go anywhere. We'll simply snuggle together and pretend we are on a trip. Our wedding trip maybe. Where do you want to go?"

She rubbed her hands over her rounded belly. "Back to bed. I'm tired. All I want is a good night's sleep without someone kicking my ribs in one spot until they ache."

"It must be a girl, then."

She tipped her head. "Why do you say that?"

"I've often found women to be a pain in my side."

She grinned at him and he smiled back. He leaned in and kissed her before she knew what was happening. "Good night. Sleep well."

He walked away into the darkness. She wanted to call him back, wanted to recapture that flicker of attraction they had shared, but she knew she shouldn't. He was kind and considerate and funny. She didn't deserve it, but she wondered if he might have feelings for her just a little.

It proved to be a short night. Gemma was up at four thirty in the morning to wash, dry and put up her hair. She was dressed in her wedding dress and white apron with her newly starched *kapp* in her hand, staring out the window, wondering what Jesse was thinking, when Anna and Bethany came in to hurry her along. Both still newlyweds, the light of happiness in their eyes gave Gemma courage. She was doing the right thing. She would be a good wife to Jesse and never give him cause to regret this day.

Bethany took Gemma's hand. "It's time. Jedidiah has the buggy here for you. Let me pin your *kapp* on."

Gemma had asked Bethany and Michael to be members of her bridal party. Jedidiah Zook was acting as *hostler*, the driver for the group. The wedding would take place at Bethany's home while Gemma's mother readied their home for the wedding meal.

Gemma nodded. She was ready, but her fingers were cold as ice. Was a father for her child reason enough to wed Jesse?

She looked in the mirror, as she made sure her *kapp* was on straight. The woman looking back at her knew the answer. The real reason she was here was because she admired the man about to become her husband and wanted to provide the warm welcoming home that he had missed out on as a child. Maybe he didn't love her, but he cared enough to want to be her husband and to call her child his own.

Bethany squeezed Gemma's hand. "It will be fine."

"How can I be sure?"

"You care for each other, don't you?" Anna asked. "Love is sure to follow. I've seen the way Jesse looks at you."

Gemma looked out the window. "Jesse says love isn't necessary to have a good marriage."

Her two friends exchanged pointed glances. Gemma didn't want them to feel sorry for her. "He's a good man."

Gemma took a deep breath. The baby was only part of the reason for this day. With God's help, she would be a good wife and a good mother. She looked down at her expanding waist and wrapped her arms across her stomach.

"What's wrong, Gemma?" Anna took a step closer.

Gemma smiled at her. "I just realized that no matter what happens with my baby, she is here with me on my wedding day."

Anna grinned. "How do you know it's going to be a girl?"

Gemma closed her eyes. "Her father said so."

Jesse was waiting for her at the foot of the stairs. He looked every bit as nervous as she felt, but he also looked wonderfully handsome in his new black suit, snowy white shirt and bow tie. He smiled and held out his hand. "Are you ready?"

She grasped his fingers tightly. "I am. Are you?"

"You are stuck with me. Who else will harvest pine bark for you?" They smiled at the shared memory. Some of their former closeness remained. She needed to hold on to his friendship and not want more.

She peered into his eyes. "We're going to be all right, aren't we?"

"I think so. I really think we are."

She wanted to believe him. Needed to believe in him. He truly cared about her and about her baby.

It was just after seven o'clock when they arrived at Bethany's home. The benches were being set up by Ivan and some of his friends. Additional seating had been rented for the day. All the downstairs rooms would be filled to overflowing with guests.

Bethany brought Gemma a chair and Jesse stood beside her. They greeted each guest as they arrived. The ceremony wouldn't take place until nine o'clock, but at eight thirty, the wedding party took their places on the benches at the front of the room, where the ceremony would be held. Gemma sat with Anna and Bethany on one side of the room, Jesse sat with Michael and Tobias on the other. Their *forgeher*—or ushers—Jenny and Ivan, made sure each guest, Amish and *Englisch*, had a place on one of the long wooden benches.

The singing began followed by sermons from her father and Samuel for almost three hours. Gemma tried to keep her mind on what was being said, but she could only think of spending the next sixty years with the man beside her. Of all the mistakes she had made in the past, this was the one thing she had to get right.

Finally, Bishop Schultz stood to address the congregation. "Brothers and sisters, we are gathered here in Christ's name for a solemn purpose. Jesse Crump and Gemma Lapp are about to make irrevocable vows. This is a most serious step and not to be taken lightly, for it is a lifelong commitment to love and cherish one another."

As the bishop continued at length, Gemma glanced at Jesse. He was sitting up straight, listening to every word. He didn't look the least bit nervous anymore. The bishop motioned for them to come forward.

Gemma knew the questions that would be asked of her and she answered them in a clear strong voice. To her relief, Jesse did the same. The bishop placed their hands together. "The God of Abraham, of Isaac and of Jacob be with you. May He bestow His blessings richly upon you through Jesus Christ, amen."

That was it. They were man and wife.

A final prayer ended the ceremony. The couple was whisked back to Gemma's home, where the women of the congregation began preparing the wedding meal in the kitchen. The men had arranged tables in a U-shape around the walls of the living room. In the corner of the room, facing the front door, the place of honor, the *eck*, meaning the corner table, was quickly set up for the wedding party.

He was married. Jesse waited for it to sink in. It hadn't yet. It didn't feel real. When the table was ready, Jesse took his place with his groomsmen seated to his right. Gemma was ushered in and took her seat at his left-hand side, symbolizing the place she would occupy in his life. A helpmate, always at his side through good times and bad. Gemma's cheeks were pale. Was the day too much for her? Under the table, he squeezed her hand. She gave him a shy smile in return.

Jesse spoke to the people who filed past. The single men among the guests were arranged along the table to his right and the single women were arranged along the tables to Gemma's left. Later, at the evening meal, the unmarried people would be paired up according to the bride and groom's choosing. Amish weddings were where matchmakings often got started, especially in a place like New Covenant where marriage-minded singles had to look far afield for mates. The non-Amish guests gathered together at tables and in groups as they wished. All the guests were invited to remain, eat and visit at their leisure by Gemma's parent.

Although most Amish wedding meals went on until long after dark, Gemma went around to bid their guests goodbye in the midafternoon. She had strict orders from her mother and the midwife to return to bed before the evening meal. She saw Jesse and her father deep in discussion. Jesse looked amazing in his new suit, and he had a smile on his face. A smile she was coming to adore, especially when it was directed at her. She decided not to bother them but to let *Mamm* know she was retiring. She looked over the crowd but didn't see her mother.

Dale crossed the room with a glass of punch in his hand and a wide grin on his face. "I can't believe the big man finally said 'I do.'"

Gemma smiled at him. "You have to take some of the credit for bringing us together, Dale."

He chuckled and raised his glass. "That's right. If I'd made it back to the truck that day, the two of you wouldn't have had a chance to get reacquainted like you did. Jesse's ended up with a pretty bride and a swell piece of property thanks to me."

"What property? Oh, did my father finally sell Jesse the land he wanted?" No wonder Jesse was grinning.

"Sold nothing. He gave it to Jesse free and clear. That's some wedding present."

A sense of unease crept over Gemma. Her heart began to pound. "My father gave it to him? Are you sure Jesse didn't buy it?"

"Jesse didn't have to spend a penny for it. You've got a real generous old man." Dale finished off his drink and gestured toward the serving table. "I'm gonna get a refill. Do you want something?"

To unhear what Dale had just told her.

Gemma's happiness drained away. She glanced to where her father and Jesse were still talking together. Her father's words echoed in her mind.

We won't have any success getting someone from here to marry her when word gets out. I'll have my brother in Lancaster find a fellow. There must be some man who will marry her once he learns he will inherit this farm one day. Had he made the same offer to Jesse, using the land Jesse wanted so badly?

Had Jesse accepted her father's offer? Was that why he had proposed? Not to give her child a name but to gain a valuable piece of land? Were his claims of affection as empty as Robert's had been?

She pressed both hands to her cheeks. It couldn't

be true. Jesse wasn't like that. There had to be another explanation. She shivered as her hands grew cold. She had trusted him.

Jesse happened to glance her way. He spoke to her father and started walking toward her. He stopped in front of her and tipped his head slightly to the side. "Are you okay?"

Ask him about it.

She shook her head. "I am going to lie down."

He took her hand. "Your fingers are like ice." He curled his large hand around hers.

Jesse held her hand as they walked up the stairs to her room. Tradition dictated that the couple would spend the night at the home of the bride's parents and help clean up from the festivities the next day. It wasn't going to be a traditional wedding night.

Jesse stopped outside her bedroom door. "Should I send someone up to stay with you?"

"*Nee*, go back down to our guests. Just because I can't be there doesn't mean you should miss it. I'm sorry your mother didn't come."

"Perhaps we can visit her after the baby is born."

Gemma nodded. "I would like that."

"You didn't get overly tired, did you?"

Was he truly concerned for her? "I feel perfectly fit, and I'm sorry I'm being sent to my room by the mean midwife. I know she has my best interest at heart."

Jesse laughed out loud. "I dare you to call her that to her face."

"I think not. It's good to see you smiling, Jesse. Are you happy?"

"I have a lot to smile about."

"You and my *daed* looked to be getting along well."

"I know you and he have had your differences, but Leroy is a generous man."

"In what way?" *Please tell me the truth.*

He cupped her chin in the palm of his hand. "He has gifted me with his lovely daughter. She is mine to have and to hold for the rest of our lives. Here's to many more smiling days for both of us." He bent down and kissed her as thoroughly as she had wanted to be kissed by him for a long time. It didn't quiet the doubt flooding her mind.

"Did you get what you wanted, Jesse?"

He looked puzzled. "What?"

"Did you get what you wanted? My father offered you land to marry me, didn't he?"

His brows grew together in a fierce frown. "What are you asking?"

"Did you marry me to get the land you wanted so badly?" Her hands grew even more ice-cold. The silence stretched so long she thought she would scream.

"Is that the kind of man you think you married?"

She raised her chin. "Tell me I'm wrong."

"First tell me why you would think the worst of me? What have I done to destroy your trust?"

"I want an answer, Jesse."

Sadness filled his eyes. "So do I." He turned away.

She wanted to call him back but couldn't. What if she had been wrong to accuse him? Why couldn't he give her a simple answer?

"I'm going back to my place tonight. I think it best I stay there," he said. "Good night, Gemma."

She turned away and went into her room. She shut the door and leaned against it as tears welled up in her eyes. What had she done?

Chapter Fourteen

Jesse jerked upright out of a sound sleep. Roscoe stood beside the bed, howling a long drawn-out wail.

"What is wrong with you? Go lie down."

Roscoe slunk from the room. Jesse dropped back to the mattress and pulled his quilt up to his chin. Without his hound howling in his ear, he caught the sound of a siren in the distance. He sat up again. Was it coming closer? Roscoe raced to the front door and started barking. Jesse rolled out of bed and quickly pulled on his clothes. He hitched his suspenders over his shoulders and reached for his coat. "Quiet."

Roscoe stopped barking and Jesse heard the clatter of hooves galloping up his lane.

He pulled open his front door just as Ivan reined his horse to a halt. The boy hadn't taken time to put on a saddle. He slid from the horse's bare back and hurried to Jesse. "It's Gemma. Dinah says to come quick. I'll hitch up your buggy."

"Don't bother. Will your horse carry double?"

"I've never tried. You take him. I'll bring your buggy."

"Fine." Jesse sat down and pulled on his boots. He

gave a quick look around, found his wallet and hurried out the door. Ivan was still holding the horse's bridle. Jesse swung up onto the animal, who shifted uneasily under the unfamiliar weight. "Easy, boy."

Ivan handed him the reins and Jess headed the animal out the lane. He hadn't ridden bareback since he was a kid. If the horse dumped him, he would be sorry he hadn't taken a buggy instead. Reassured by the knowledge that Ivan would be coming behind him soon, he pushed the horse to a gallop on the snowy roadway.

Gemma must have gone into labor. How was she? Was the baby okay, or was it already too late? He prayed that God would spare both of them.

He shouldn't have been so angry with her. He could have easily said he turned down her father's offer, but would she have believed him? That she had questioned his honor and his motives hurt deeply, but none of that mattered now. She had to be okay.

He saw the flashing red lights of the ambulance reflected off the snow up ahead before he turned onto the highway. The siren stopped. They must have reached the Lapp farm. His horse tried to make the turn into Michael's lane and almost unseated Jesse. He was able to regain control and keep the animal on the highway, but he slowed his headlong gallop. The ambulance crew didn't need to pick up another patient.

Jesse drew the horse to a stop in front of the Lapp house. One of Gemma's cousins, he couldn't remember the young woman's name, took the horse's reins. "I've got him. Go on in."

"How is she?"

"I don't know." She led the skittish horse away.

Jesse strode into the house. Everyone was up and

milling in the living room. Leroy stood by the stair-
case, looking upward. Jesse laid a hand on his shoulder. "What happened?"

"We heard her cry out. Dinah ran upstairs and then
shouted for me to call an ambulance. We forgot Gemma
had a phone. I ran down to the phone shanty and made
the call. It seemed to take them forever to get here."

"Can I go up?"

"The ambulance fellow said to keep the area clear. I
think you should wait here. I'm so sorry for the way I
treated her when she first came home. You were right.
I didn't treasure my own child as I should have." He
turned away, wiping tears from his eyes.

It was the longest fifteen minutes of Jesse's life. Finally, the men in uniforms appeared at the top of the
stairs with a stretcher and quickly made their way down.
Jesse caught sight of Gemma's pale face. Her freckles
stood out in sharp contrast against her white skin. Her
eyes were closed. "Gemma, it's Jesse. I'm here. You're
going to be fine." He didn't know if she could hear him.

One of the men held an IV bag in his teeth as he maneuvered the stretcher off the stairs. Michael appeared
beside Jesse. He took the bag and held it high.

"Thanks, buddy. Is the husband here?"

"I'm her husband. How is she?" Jesse asked, fear-
ing the answer.

"We're gonna have to talk on the way. You can ride
with us."

Leroy and Dinah held on to each other as the
stretcher went past them. "Send us word," Leroy said
as Jesse met his gaze.

"I will as soon as I can."

Bethany pushed a cell phone into his hand. "Esther's

number is in here. Contact her and she'll get a message to us."

After Gemma's stretcher was secured, Jesse got in beside her and the driver quickly closed the doors. The siren came on as the ambulance drove down the lane.

"What can you tell me about your wife's condition?" One of the men was listening to her heart while the other one was waiting for Jesse's answer.

"She has a partial placenta previa." Jesse did some quick math in his head. "The baby is twenty-nine weeks gestation."

He continued to answer questions when what he really wanted was answers of his own. "How is the baby?"

"We still have fetal heart tones, so that's good. Your wife is losing a lot of blood. She will likely go straight into surgery for a cesarean when we get to the hospital. They aren't equipped to care for premature babies for an extended time. If needed, a helicopter will be on the way from Bangor, and your baby will likely be transferred to the neonatal unit there."

Jesse nodded, trying to take in the information being given to him, but his eyes were glued to the machine over her head with bouncing lines moving across it. He knew it was Gemma's heartbeat, but he had no idea if it was normal.

He took hold of her limp hand. Her fingers were cold. He wanted to tuck them inside his shirt to warm them. It was a helpless feeling, knowing everything was out of his control.

The ambulance pulled into the emergency bay and the back doors were pulled open. Gemma was unloaded and wheeled into the hospital. He tried to follow but he was stopped by a security officer. "Your wife is being well taken care of. I need you to step over to the counter and give us some info."

Jesse gave them all the information he could. When he was finished, a volunteer took him to the surgical waiting room. He was the only one in it. Suddenly the pressure and worry of the day caught up with him. He sat abruptly on the couch as his legs gave out. They had to be okay. Both of them. He needed both of them.

Please, Lord, show mercy to my wife and to her child. They are in Your hands. Guide those who care for them that they may do Your will.

He sat and prayed silently for the two most important people in his life.

About twenty minutes later, he heard a commotion. He stepped to the door to check the hallway. Several people in hospital garb walked by. The piece of equipment they were pushing turned out to be an incubator. They went past him and through the doors leading to the surgery area.

It was a good sign that they needed an incubator, wasn't it? There wasn't anyone he could ask. Another twenty minutes went by and the group came out again. One of the women smiled at him. "Are you Jesse Crump?"

"I am."

"Would you like to meet your daughter?"

"Is she okay?" Joy nearly choked him.

"Come see for yourself."

He walked timidly toward them, not knowing what to expect. The woman moved aside so he could see into the incubator. He stared at Gemma's baby through the clear top. She was amazing. And beautiful. He had never seen such a tiny child. His finger was thicker than her scrawny legs. Her head was covered with thick brown hair that had a red tint to it.

"She has so much hair for an early baby."

"In my twenty years as a delivery nurse, I've never seen a preemie without a head of hair."

He smiled as he gazed at Gemma's daughter. Her face was heart shaped with a tiny bow mouth. There were wrinkles on her forehead that made him think of Gemma when she was angry. Taped to the side of her face was a clear tube with prongs that fitted in her nose.

The baby's eyes were closed. He couldn't tell their color, but her eyelashes were long and curved where they lay against her cheeks. Awed by the wonder of this new life, he knew without a doubt that she was God's greatest gift to him.

"You look like your mother," he told her.

She opened her eyes and blinked owlishly. Then she let out a hearty wail, letting the world know she had arrived. A wonderful warmth filled his chest as he fell head over heels in love with the most beautiful child he had ever laid eyes on.

He spoke to the doctor without taking his eyes off his child. "Is she going to be okay?"

"The steroids your wife received allowed her lungs to mature. She's getting a small amount of oxygen, but she is doing amazingly well for her size. She weighs three pounds and five ounces."

"A sack of sugar weighs more," he mused.

"We are taking her to Bangor to the NICU there. We don't have room for you on the helicopter, but we can arrange transportation to get you to the NICU today. She is ten weeks premature, but all her vital signs look good at the moment. A lot will depend on how well she does in the next forty-eight hours."

"We should get going," the nurse said. "Would you like to hold her hand before we go?"

He nodded. She opened one of the round windows in the side. Another nurse gave him some foam to rub on his hands. When it was dry, he reached in and touched his little girl. He laid his finger on her palm and she immediately grabbed hold of him. "You're strong. God be with you. I'll see you soon. Don't forget me."

The nurse closed the window. "Barring any serious complications, I like to tell the family to expect their baby to go home close to her due date."

"She might be in the hospital another ten weeks?"

"Give or take a few days, yes. Babies don't grow and mature any faster outside Mom than they do inside."

He would certainly need help from his community and others to cover her hospital bill, but he was not worried about the money. He would pay what he could. The bishop would collect alms to cover the rest. If it was more than the community could provide, a call would go out to all Amish communities to render assistance.

He looked at the doctor. "How is Gemma?"

"She lost a lot of blood, but they were able to stop the bleeding. She may be in the hospital for several days longer than normal."

The elevator doors opened, and he watched as they wheeled Gemma's daughter inside.

"Does she have a name?" the nurse asked.

He and Gemma had not discussed a name for the child. It seemed odd now to think how seldom Gemma had spoken about the baby. He glanced at the door.

Did the baby look like her father? Only Gemma could answer that question. He hadn't given much thought to Robert, but he did now. Somewhere there was a man who didn't know that he had a daughter. One who hadn't been given the chance to see his beautiful child. If Gemma was right, the man willingly gave up any claim to his baby. Jesse would pray for him.

He looked at the nurse. "I will let her mother decide on a name."

"That's fine. I left some paperwork on Mom's chart. It has our contact information. Feel free to call and check on your daughter anytime of the day or night."

The elevator doors closed. He rubbed a hand over his face. The baby was okay. That was what everyone would want to know. Now he needed to see his wife.

He went back to the waiting room and got out the phone Bethany had given him. He dialed Esther's number. She answered on the second ring. He spent the next ten minutes updating her and having her relay messages to Gemma's family. When he hung up, a young man in green scrubs came into the waiting room. "You must be Jesse Crump." He held out his hand. "I am Dr. Brentwood. I have just finished surgery on your wife."

Jesse shook his hand. "How is Gemma? Can I see her?"

"She had a rough go of it, but I anticipate a full recovery. She needed several units of blood. Your wife will be in recovery for the next two hours. You'll be able to see her after that."

"Thank you, Dr. Brentwood. I appreciate everything you have done."

Knowing that he had two hours to wait, Jesse went in search of a cup of coffee and something to eat. When he reached the lobby, he saw a green van stop outside. A half-dozen women wearing Amish clothing began getting out. He recognized Gemma's mother and her cousins who had attended the wedding.

Two of them carried large quilted bags over their arms. Dinah caught sight of him and hurried toward him. The other women followed her. They crowded around, asking about Gemma.

"She is in recovery. She will be there for another two hours. After that, she will be moved to a room. We will be able to see her then."

"Where can we wait?" one of her cousins asked.

He showed them to the waiting area. Dinah opened the bag she carried and withdrew several wrapped sandwiches. "I thought you might be hungry."

Someone else produced a thermos of hot coffee and disposable cups. He drank the coffee and tried to eat a sandwich, but he was too worried about Gemma. Her baby had been whisked away in a helicopter before she had even laid eyes on her. He knew that would be upsetting.

"Did you see the baby before they took her away?" Dinah asked.

"I did." He proceeded to tell them about Gemma's baby. He remembered her weight, but he didn't remember being told how long she was. They plied him for information until Dinah gently asked them to let him swallow a bite of his sandwich.

The time passed more quickly with company. He was surprised when a nurse came out to tell him he could see Gemma. He bolted out of his chair and followed her.

She lay on pristine white sheets. He thought her color was better than when she had left the house on the stretcher, but she was still pale. And beautiful. Tears filled his eyes as he pulled up a chair beside her bed. "Gemma. Open your eyes. Can you hear me, darling? It's Jesse."

Gemma heard Jesse's voice, but she couldn't make her eyes open. There was something important she needed to know. Something she had to ask him. She struggled again to open her eyes and he was there.

"Jesse?" Her voice came out scratchy and hoarse.

"Time to wake up, sleepyhead."

"Not yet." She drifted off for a few seconds and then opened her eyes wide. "The baby?"

"She's fine."

"A girl?"

"We have a *dochtah.*"

"A daughter. You said it would be a girl. Where is she?" Gemma tried to raise her head. It was too heavy. She let it fall back. "Can I see her?"

"I'm afraid you can't see her yet." His voice held an odd quality that scared her.

"Why not? Why can't I see her? What's wrong?" She struggled to rise.

He gently restrained her. "Take it easy. She wasn't due for another two months, remember? She is premature. They can't take care of her at this hospital, so they have taken her to another one."

"Where?"

"Bangor."

"That's so far. She's all alone." A tear slipped from the corner of her eye.

"She isn't alone. She has some wonderful nurses and doctors taking care of her."

"That's not the same. Are you sure she is okay?" She raised her hand and he took hold of it. He was so strong and so gentle. If only she could believe that his affection was real.

"I saw her before they took her away and she was hollering at the top of her lungs."

"That's *goot*, isn't it?"

"Very *goot*."

Gemma cringed with the rising pain. "She needs you, Jesse. You have to be with her."

"We will go see her together," he coaxed.

"*Nee*, you have to protect her. She needs you."

He bent close. "You need me here."

"I do, but she needs you more. Promise you'll go."

"I promise. Now, get some rest."

"Okay." Gemma closed her eyes and let her mind float away. *Why did you marry me, Jesse?*

Chapter Fifteen

By late that afternoon, Jesse was in Bangor at the medical center. Dale had been able to drive him, and Jesse was grateful to the bishop for arranging it. He went through the routine of filling out paperwork at the admissions office and then was asked to wait until a volunteer escort could show him to the nursery. All the while, his mind kept jumping back to Gemma. Was she doing okay? Was she in much pain?

He was torn between the need to be with his new wife and the desire to be with his new daughter. Gemma had insisted that he come to protect the baby. He didn't know what he could do that couldn't be done by the nurses and staff taking care of her but if his being here relieved Gemma's mind, he would make the long trip as often as she wanted him to.

An elderly man in a pink jacket arrived to show Jesse the way. As they walked together along a lengthy hall, the man cast a sidelong glance at him. "Are you Amish or Mennonite?"

"Amish."

"There aren't many of you folks this far north."

"There are more coming every year. The price of your farmland is reasonable and that makes Maine attractive to us."

"Are you a potato farmer?"

"I am. In the off-season, I build garden sheds and tiny houses at a business near my farm."

"I grew up on a potato farm. I'm old enough to remember my grandfather farming with horses. It's nice to see that coming back."

"Many of our *Englisch* neighbors in New Covenant feel the same way."

They stopped at an elevator and got on when the doors opened. The man selected the floor and pushed the button.

"I'm going to take you as far as the NICU doors," he said when the elevator stopped. He pointed the way, and Jesse stepped out. A receptionist sat behind a glassed-in desk. She opened a set of double doors and beckoned him inside. He followed her into the nursery, where she showed him how to scrub his hands up to his elbows and informed him he would do this every time he came in. He was willing to do whatever it took to safeguard his child.

Another nurse was summoned. She was a tall girl with a long black ponytail. She introduced herself as Jill and said she was Baby Crump's nurse. Her calm and friendly demeanor went a long way to soothe his worries.

At his daughter's bedside, he stopped in surprise when he saw the jumble of wires that were hooked to her. She was still wearing her oxygen tubing, but she was just as beautiful as he remembered. She lay on an open bed with a heating unit above her. An IV hung from a pole on a small machine that hummed and clicked softly. A white bandage on her arm held the IV in place. Behind her, a screen displayed several bouncing red lines and a lot of numbers that meant nothing to him. He stared at them, trying to make sense of what they were telling him.

"Mothers gaze at their baby's face. Fathers spend more time watching the monitors," Jill said with a chuckle.

"Then they must understand what the numbers mean because I don't," he admitted. "How is she doing?"

"Very well. She has some mild breathing problems, but the oxygen she is on is a small amount. Is her mother going to be nursing her or using formula?"

"I believe she will nurse her, but I don't know for sure. It will be several days before she can come here."

"It is almost her feeding time. Would you like to hold her?"

Excitement made him giddy. "Of course I would." His elation took a quick dive, tempered by uncertainty. "Are you sure it's okay?"

Smiling, Jill patted his arm. "I'll be right here. Have you heard of kangaroo care?"

He shook his head. "What does an Australian animal have to do with human babies?"

"That is what we call it when parents hold their baby skin to skin. We'll lay her on your bare chest and cover her with a blanket. Your body heat will keep her warm. The sound of your heartbeat will soothe her. We have found premature babies gain more weight and grow better with this type of contact. Want to try it?"

"Sure."

"We ask that you hold her for at least an hour. Do you have that much time today?"

"I have all the time she needs."

Jill grinned. "I like your attitude. I need to get her feeding ready."

The baby lay on her side with both hands tucked under her chin. He leaned in to speak softly to her. "*Goot* morn, *Liebchen*. Do you remember me? I'm your *daed*. Your father. I get to hold you today. Would you like that?"

Her eyes fluttered open at the sound of his voice, and she yawned.

Jill chuckled as she came back with the syringe filled with what he assumed was infant formula. "I don't think she's as eager as you are."

She indicated a recliner beside the bed. "Okay, Jesse, unbutton your shirt."

Feeling self-conscious, he sat still as a stone in the chair while the nurses transferred the babe. One of her wires came loose. Alarms sounded. He looked to Jill, who smiled reassuringly. "Just a loose lead. She's fine." She laid the baby on his chest and reconnected her to the monitor. The steady *beep, beep, beep* was comforting.

His large hands covered his daughter's entire body. She lay light as a feather against him. A rush of emotion filled his heart to overflowing, making it hard to breathe. Jill laid a warm blanket over the two of them, and the babe proceeded to make herself comfortable. She wiggled against his skin, her tiny fingers grasping handfuls of his chest hair. It was an amazing feeling, having her tiny warm body next to his heart. He wanted to hold on to this marvelous moment forever. He was holding Gemma's daughter. His daughter. It was everything he had imagined it would be and more.

Could she hear his heartbeat? Did she recall the sound of her mother's beating heart? Sadness settled over him, dulling his happiness. He looked up at Jill standing close by. "It should be her mother holding her for the first time."

"Her mother held her safe and close for all these past months. It's okay for Dad to take his turn. Would you like me to take a picture for you?"

He considered her offer carefully. "If you make sure my face is not seen it will be acceptable. I'm sure her mother will want to know what she looks like."

As eager as he had been to see and hold his child, he was just as eager to get back to Gemma. Hopefully all of them would soon be together. He looked up when a man in a white coat stopped in front of him. He introduced himself as the baby's neonatologist and proceeded to update Jesse on the things that they were watching. It wasn't as good of a report as Jesse had been hoping to hear.

On the following morning, Gemma was sitting up in the chair for the first time when Jesse walked in. Relief and delight swirled through her body before she could tamp down her emotions. She wanted to fling herself into his arms, but she knew that wasn't going to happen. "How is she? I miss her so much and I've never even seen her face."

"I can help with that." He pulled a chair over to her and sat down. He wanted to kiss her; the need to hold her close burned in his chest but he didn't want to hurt her. He settled for a quick peck on her cheek when he was sure no one was watching. Public displays of affection between Amish adults, even married ones, were frowned upon. He longed to tell her how much she had come to mean to him, but the uncertainty between them kept him silent.

He took out his wallet and carefully removed the photograph Jill had taken of their baby. Only Jesse's fingers were visible in it. Gemma's hands shook as she took it and gazed at it with a look of endearing tenderness. Then slowly the joy in her eyes dimmed. "What's on her face? What's wrong with her arm? Is it broken?"

He had become accustomed to seeing the baby with all her tubing and equipment. He had to remember that Gemma had not seen any of it. "The little tube in her nose is giving her oxygen. That white bandage on her arm is to keep her from pulling her IV out. The blue tube in her mouth goes to her stomach. That's the way they feed her right now. When she gets a little bigger, they will use a bottle until you can nurse her. Isn't she beautiful? Her hair has hints of red in it. Her eyes are blue, but they told me all babies have blue eyes. I think she looks like you."

"You never met Robert. She isn't fine, is she? She's sick. They wouldn't be giving her oxygen if she was fine."

He had been trying hard to make it sound positive, but Gemma was right. "She's needing a little more oxygen today. Her blood levels show she may need a transfusion. They say it's not unexpected, and they still believe she's doing well. They just have to keep a close eye on her."

"You should be there. Why did you come back?"

"To see my wife. To bring her a picture of her daughter. I'm sure the bishop won't object to one photograph in a situation like ours. They are taking good care of her."

Gemma closed her eyes and nodded slightly. Was he telling the truth or trying to spare her? "I'm sorry. It was kind of you to think of me. I'm tired, that's all. Would you call the nurse to help me back to bed?"

"Sure thing." He rose and stepped out into the hall until he located a staff member. He waited outside the room while they moved her. Once she was back in bed, the nurse's aide opened the door. Gemma heard someone call his name. Michael, Bethany and Anna were coming toward her room. Ivan and Jenny followed behind them with a pair of bright pink balloons in hand. It's a Girl was written in gold lettering. Her parents came behind the children.

Gemma blinked away the moisture in her eyes. How could she tell her friends and family it was too soon to celebrate the birth of her baby? She couldn't. She would smile, thank them and keep her deep fear hidden from everyone, including Jesse. She was terrified her daughter was going to die.

Four days later, when Gemma was released from the hospital, she and Jesse made the long trip to Bangor with plans to stay for a week and perhaps longer in the accommodations the hospital provided for families with infants in the NICU. Jesse kept a close eye on Gemma. She was quiet and withdrawn. He worried that the trip was too much for her so soon after surgery.

She never complained, so he had little evidence to base his feelings on. Something just wasn't right.

When they were settled in the guest rooms, he went

to the kitchenette and fixed them both a cup of hot tea. He offered it to Gemma. "It's not rose hip tea, but it's okay."

She accepted her cup gratefully. "It's hot and that's what counts. Our marriage isn't off to a very good start. You must regret marrying me."

"Of course I don't. I have a beautiful new daughter. Jill is going to ask me if we have picked a name for her yet. Shall we decide before we go over to visit her?"

"I'm not up to a visit just yet." She put her cup down.

Was she feeling worse than she was letting on? "That's fine. What about the name?"

"I won't know until I see her face. The picture was nice but seeing her in person will be best."

"That I understand. Can I do anything for you before I go over to visit her?"

She kept her gaze down. "I'm fine, Jesse. Stop worrying about me."

"If you say so."

"I didn't marry you to become a burden."

"You will never be a burden to me." He bent to kiss her cheek. "Get some rest."

She nodded meekly.

After he left their room, he stopped in the hospital lobby and placed a call to the phone shanty for Gemma's mother. He was worried that Gemma seemed detached from the baby. The NICU nurse had mentioned it happened occasionally when mothers didn't bond with their infants at birth. He left a message telling his in-laws that they had arrived safely and he would call again with an update tomorrow.

Jill was sitting beside his daughter's bed, writing on

a chart when he came in. She looked up with a wide smile. "Your little one is off oxygen as of this morning."

"That's great." He couldn't stop his wide grin.

"Where is her mother? I've been looking forward to meeting her."

His smile faded. "The trip wore her out. She'll be in later."

Jill put down her pen and leaned on her writing desk. "Poor thing. What a rough delivery she has had. She'll feel better when she sees the baby."

"What else is new with my girl?"

"She's two ounces above her birth weight. To celebrate, I was going to make a card for her mother. I hate to ask, but do we have a name?"

He thought about it for a second. "Hope."

Gemma could change it if she wanted but that was how he saw this child. A gift of hope.

"Aw, I like that. It's not her feeding time, so you aren't going to be able to hold her."

"That's okay. I can admire her from afar."

Gemma woke in near-total darkness with her heart pounding in terror. Only a faint glow shone under the door of the bedroom. It took her a few seconds to figure out where she was. At the hospital in Bangor in one of the rooms reserved for parents of sick babies.

She checked the other bed and saw Jesse was sleeping sprawled across it. She eased out of bed and slipped her dressing gown over her long nightgown. She pulled her braid from beneath her gown and let it fall down her back. Her slippers were at the foot of the bed. She wiggled her feet into them and quietly left the suite. She had to get to the nursery. Her baby girl was dying.

.The elevator seemed to take forever, but it finally opened on the correct floor. She spoke to the receptionist, who opened the door for her. Inside the unit, she had no idea where to go. She rushed over to the first nurse she saw. "Where's my baby? Is she gone already? Please tell me."

"Tell me your name and we'll see where your baby is."

"Gemma Lapp. I mean Crump."

"Ah, little Hope's mommy. Your baby is right over here." She led the way to where a babe with thick reddish-brown hair lay sleeping in an incubator. Gemma leaned close. Was this the same infant in the photograph? Had Jesse named her? Gemma looked at the nurse. "This is my baby?"

"Yes."

"Can I touch her?"

"First, I have to show you how to wash up. Then you can have a seat and I'll let you hold her."

"I woke up and thought something was wrong. I had to come see."

"A nightmare? They can feel so real sometimes. I'm Pepper. I'll be Hope's nurse until the day shift comes on. Where is Jesse?"

"I didn't wake him."

"He is such a good father. I wish there were more like him."

Gemma eased into a rocking chair. "I've never held her before."

Pepper opened the side of the incubator, deftly wrapped the babe in two blankets and laid her in Gemma's arms.

It was almost like holding nothing and the whole world at the same time. Gemma pulled the blankets aside to see her better. After gazing at her face, she started checking all her fingers and her tiny feet. "You're okay, aren't you? I had such a bad dream about you, but you're okay. My beautiful, beautiful baby girl. My Hope."

Gemma closed the blanket around her, so she wouldn't be cold. "I was afraid to meet you. Isn't that silly? You aren't a punishment. You're a pearl beyond compare. Look at your cute ears and your nose. I love every inch of you."

"She is a special gift from God to us."

Gemma looked up to see Jesse smiling at her. "She's amazing, Jesse. I didn't know."

He knelt beside her and cupped the baby's head. Gemma laid her hand over his. "Thank you."

"For what?" he asked, looking puzzled.

"For taking care of her while I couldn't."

"You are most welcome."

She gazed at her baby and then looked into Jesse's eyes. No matter why he had married her, she was in his debt. She wouldn't burden him with unwanted affection or question his motives. She would do all she could to give him a happy home, even if he never loved her. "I will be a good wife to you, Jesse."

He gazed at the floor for a long moment, then looked up. "Gemma, about the quarrel we had on our wedding night…"

She reached out and laid her fingers on his lips. "It doesn't matter. We are wedded, for better or for worse. Hope is who matters now."

He nodded and gave a half-hearted smile. It didn't erase the concern she saw in her eyes.

Chapter Sixteen

Jesse put in a call to update Gemma's parents and to ask for help. It produced immediate results. Dinah, Bethany and Anna arrived later that day to stay with and support Gemma. He was thrilled that she was bonding with Hope, but Gemma still wasn't herself. He put it down to the strain of the situation, but it didn't ease his mind completely. What was he missing?

She had become the most important person in his life. Was he in love with her? He wanted her to be happy. To smile and laugh and bicker with him the way she had when he gave her a tour of his home. Maybe he was being impatient. Maybe time was all she needed.

Remembering his vow to love and cherish his wife gave him solace. She needed her family and her baby now. Once life returned to normal, he and Gemma would have a lifetime to grow close once more. He longed to hear her say she loved him, but he was the one who had insisted love wasn't necessary in their marriage. He would wait until Hope was home and thriving before he asked Gemma for something she might not be able to give him. Her love.

On the following Monday, they all returned to New Covenant, leaving Hope in the skilled and kind hands of the NICU staff. Jesse needed to return to work. He faced rapidly mounting medical bills.

Gemma fought back tears as she left her baby. She barely spoke on the ride home, and he knew she was missing her baby. On Tuesday she seemed better, but he could tell she was still depressed. They were both staying with her parents as was the custom for Amish newlyweds, but he had his own room. Gemma needed all the rest she could get. Her mother made sure she got it. He was glad for the added help in keeping Gemma's mind occupied while he was at work.

On Wednesday morning, Dinah caught him in the hall before Gemma was up. "I'm going to suggest a shopping trip to Gemma today. I want you to support the idea."

Did his wife enjoy shopping? He didn't know. The dwindling balance in his bank account gave him pause but if it helped Gemma, he wouldn't refuse. "A *goot* idea. Would you like me to take you?"

"I'll have Michael drive us. He mentioned he needed to go into town today and he has the patience needed to wait in the buggy while I'm in a store."

Jesse grinned. "Is this something I should cultivate?"

"Most definitely. We're going shopping for baby clothes and essentials. Gemma needs a gentle reminder that Hope will be home soon. She needs to concentrate on the future instead of bemoaning the fact that she doesn't have her child with her now."

"You've been a blessing to me, Dinah." Much more than his own mother, who hadn't come to the wedding or even acknowledged it.

"My *sohn*, you have been a blessing to me. More than you will know until you become a *grossdaadi*. When I looked upon the face of my grandchild, I knew it was God's way of giving me a glimpse into the joy that awaits me when I am called to my final home."

"I pray that is many years away." He folded his arms across his chest and stared at the floor as he framed his next question. "Does it bother you that I am not Hope's true father?"

When Dinah didn't answer, he looked up. She was smiling. She patted his cheek. "I forgot that. *Nee*, it bothers me not one bit. This is the last time we will think upon it, *ja*?"

"*Ja*," he agreed as his heart grew light. "Have fun shopping and bring a smile to Gemma's face if you can."

When his wife and Dinah left, he stopped by Bethany's and asked her to come with him to see Anna. When they were gathered around Anna's kitchen table, he sat forward in his chair and glanced between Anna and Bethany. "Have you noticed anything different about Gemma? Something that's not quite right?"

The two women exchanged speaking looks. Bethany nodded. "We have."

Anna laid her hands on the table. "*Subdued* is perhaps the word."

"Do either of you know what's going on?" he asked.

"Baby blues? She is going through a difficult time. You both are," Anna said quietly.

He nodded. "The midwife mentioned I should let her know if Gemma seems depressed. Maybe it is just the blues." That would get better with time.

"Have you told Gemma that you love her?" Bethany asked.

He shifted uncomfortably in his chair. "Not in so many words. I care for her and she knows that."

Bethany stabbed a finger in the air toward him. "You care for her. She *loves* you."

He sat up to stare at her. "Has she said this?"

Bethany relaxed her attitude. "Not in so many words, but I know my friend."

He glanced between the two women. "Why wouldn't she tell me how she felt?"

"Because yours wasn't a love match in the beginning, and you don't think love is necessary for a good marriage. Isn't that what you told her?"

"I admit I might not have known what I was talking about when I said it."

Anna nodded. "That's a smart answer. Remember, Gemma may be dealing with a lot of guilt too. I've read that mothers of premature babies often feel they are to blame for the early births. You saved Gemma's life in the storm. You married her to give her babe a name. You took Hope into your heart like she was your own. Gemma may not feel worthy of your affections."

He blew out a slow breath. "What do I do?"

The two women exchanged glances. Anna gave a slight shake of her head.

"What? Tell me," he insisted.

"Gemma married and became a mother all in one day," Bethany said. "She never had a chance to enjoy being alone with you. Her marriage was more of a contract than a courtship, and every woman wants to be courted, to be made to feel special by the man she adores. I'm not saying start a courtship now. You both have a lot on your plates, but when the time is right, you should set out to make her feel special."

"I have my work cut out for me, don't I?"

Bethany patted his hand. "I think you are up to the challenge."

Was courting his wife what he had to do to earn her love? He would try anything to regain their easy friendship and then let her know how much she had come to mean to him.

On her way back from their shopping trip, Gemma stopped off to see Bethany while Michael took her mother home. Bethany was scrubbing out her sink. Her bright smile lifted Gemma's spirits.

Gemma placed her packages on the table. "You have to see the cute clothes I found for Hope. It's hard to find preemie clothes. We had to go all over. I bought some material to make her a few outfits too. I know she'll outgrow them quickly."

"Did you enjoy yourself?" Bethany dried her hands on her apron.

Gemma thought about it for a second. "I did."

Bethany shook a finger at her. "I'm glad you're getting back to your old self. We were worried."

"I didn't realize I was worrying people. Who is *we*?"

"Your husband stopped in to ask Anna and me if we knew what was wrong with you."

Gemma spread out the first tiny pink dress. That Jesse was worried enough to seek the council of her friends surprised her. "I guess I've been worried about Hope. So many things could go wrong. She's so tiny."

"Is that all?"

"What else could it be?"

"That you are unhappily married?"

Gemma looked at her friend. "Don't think that. Jesse is a wonderful father, but…"

Bethany's eyes were full of sympathy. "But what?"

"He doesn't love me." Gemma shrugged. "That's the way things are and I have to accept that."

"My observation is that Jesse cares a lot about you. He wasn't faking that happy smile at his wedding."

"Maybe he had more things to smile about than getting married."

"What's that supposed to mean?"

"Never mind."

Gemma was too embarrassed to share what she suspected. Her father had practically sold her to Jesse. Was she worth eighty acres in Jesse's mind? At least something good had come out of their marriage for him. She managed a smile for her friend. "I'm going to make a few dresses for Hope out of this material. Do you like it?"

On her way home from her visit, Gemma stopped at the phone shanty and placed a call to the NICU. She was happy when Jill came on the line. "How is Hope today?"

"She's okay, except for a stuffy nose."

"Did she gain weight?"

"Let me look… No, her weight stayed the same."

"But she has been gaining every day." Concern inched its way into Gemma's mind. "Is it something serious?"

"Having a baby in an NICU is like riding a roller coaster. There are ups and downs. It's normal. Are you still planning on being here this weekend?"

"We are, and I'm going to stay until Hope is released." She wasn't going to be hours away if something did go wrong.

"That's good news. Hope will be happy to have her mommy here. Is Jesse staying too?"

"Ah, no. He has to work."

"Still, he'll feel better knowing you are with your daughter."

Gemma hoped that would be the case.

That evening she was packing her suitcase when Jesse came up to her room at her parents' home after work. She added some of the outfits she and her mother had purchased and the few she had sewn.

Jesse grinned. "She can't wear that many clothes in a weekend."

"I'm taking enough along for a month."

He looked puzzled. "For a month?"

She closed the top of her suitcase. "I'm going to stay there until she is ready to come home."

"I can understand why you want to do it."

"Bethany said you were worried because I have been depressed. I'm fine now. Oh, wait, I know how much you hate that word. I am feeling much less sad, and I'm eager to learn how to take care of my daughter. We can call each other every day."

She raised her chin, daring him to refuse to let her go. "I am going, and it doesn't matter what you say. You told me you admire people who speak the truth."

"I do. I will miss you."

It was nice to hear, but was it the truth? She picked up her nightgown and added it to the suitcase. "I will miss you too."

"Are you sure you want to do this?"

"What's the harm? If I get homesick, I'll come home."

"Then you should do what you need to do. I'll pack my things for this weekend and call for a ride."

* * *

Gemma's plan to stay with Hope for the next month or more surprised him. It would be good for both mother and babe; it made sense, but how would he and Gemma improve their relationship with so much physical distance between them? One phone call a day wasn't going to be enough. He wanted Gemma near him. He needed her. If only she believed that he had married her because he cared for her and not to gain land. How could he convince her?

On their arrival in the NICU in Bangor that evening, they were greeted with the distressing news that Hope's cold had worsened. Jill met them with a sober face. "We have had to move her into the isolation room. She has RSV. It's a viral infection that would be a cold for you or me but in premature babies, it can be very serious."

A chill ran through Jesse's body. Hope had come so far, but she was still so tiny. She didn't deserve a setback.

"Can we see her?" Gemma asked.

"Of course, but you will have to put on a gown, gloves and a mask." Jill led the way and Jesse followed, holding Gemma's hand. He knew by her grip that she was as worried as he was.

Hope was crying pitifully when they entered the special room designed to keep any contamination from spreading to the other babies. Gemma immediately went to soothe Hope and lift her out of her crib. The baby quieted, but she was still breathing hard. Her rib cage sank in as she struggled with each breath. Gemma gave Jesse a fear-filled look. It mirrored the dread in his heart.

Throughout the next two days, Jesse and Gemma held their daughter almost continuously. Being upright made the baby's breathing easier. She didn't fuss as much when she received her breathing treatments if someone was holding her. Jesse's heart broke each time she looked at him with her sad tired eyes. When the time came for him to leave, he sat holding Hope while Gemma was washing her hands.

After putting on her gloves, she stood aside. Jesse got out of the rocker and gently transferred Hope into Gemma's arms. She said, "Come here, my precious *bobbli*."

He dropped to one knee beside the chair and laid a hand on Hope's soft hair. "I can't leave, Gemma. She's not getting better. I'm worried about you too. You won't get enough rest if I'm not here to spell you."

"As much as you dislike the word *fine*, that's what I am today. Fine. My incision has healed. I'm getting stronger every day. I'm fine."

"That may be, but I'm not fine leaving you here alone. Marriage is a partnership. We will get through this together." He dropped a kiss on Hope's head.

"You love her, don't you, Jesse?" Gemma asked quietly.

"More than I ever thought possible. But you know how I feel, don't you?" He gazed into Gemma's eyes intently.

"I do. It's amazing—isn't it?—how much space someone so small can take up in your heart."

"And how much space is left over for the other people we love." He grew serious. Was now the time to tell her how he felt? "Gemma, I—"

One of Hope's alarms began ringing. Jesse looked at her monitor. He had learned the meaning of all the numbers and waving lines during Hope's first week in the unit. Most of the time, it was simply a false alarm that a wiggling baby could generate just by moving.

The monitor was over Gemma's head. She couldn't see the numbers. "What is it?"

"Her oxygen level is too low."

"Check to see if the lead is loose."

He did. It was secure. He could see the baby's lips turning blue as her numbers fell. Before he could call out, several nurses rushed to the bedside. One of them scooped Hope out of Gemma's arms and laid her in her crib. A few seconds later, a doctor hurried in. He listened to Hope with his stethoscope and scowled. "Call respiratory care. Have a ventilator brought in. We are going to intubate. Mom and Dad, I'm afraid you are going to have to step out."

"What's wrong?" Gemma demanded as Jesse helped her to her feet.

The doctor covered Hope's face with an oxygen mask. "We're going get an X-ray to be sure, but it sounds like her RSV has progressed to pneumonia. She's going to need help breathing."

A nurse touched Jesse's arm. "Please come with me. We'll take good care of her and let you come back in when we're done."

Jesse drew Gemma away with an arm across her shoulders. Outside the unit, the nurse indicated a waiting room. It was empty at the moment. Gemma turned her face into Jesse's chest and burst into sobs. He wrapped his arms tightly around her. "It's going to be okay. She's a strong girl."

Was he trying to reassure Gemma or himself? What was going on? How long before someone came to tell them something? He heard Gemma muttering prayers under her breath. He closed his eyes and prayed harder than he had ever prayed in his life.

After ten minutes of uncertainty, Jesse coaxed Gemma to sit down on the red sofa against the wall. There was a television playing in the corner, but Gemma ignored it. She dried her eyes and stared at the door. "I wish someone would tell us what's going on."

She heard the hum of a motor growing closer. The portable X-ray machine came down the hall, guided by a young woman. She pushed a button on the wall and went into the unit when the doors opened.

Jesse strode out into the hall to gaze into the unit until the doors swung shut again. He came back into the waiting room.

She looked at him hopefully. "Did you see anything?"

"Just a group of people around her bed." He sat beside Gemma. She wanted to be back in his embrace but didn't know how to ask.

She noticed his hands were clenched into tight fists. She laid her palm on one.

"I want to fight this battle for her too."

He leaned forward with his elbows on his knees and covered his face with his hands. A ragged sob broke free. Gemma threw her arms around him. If she needed comfort, he needed it too. "Don't cry, darling."

She drew his head to her shoulder. He wrapped his arms around her as his body shook with silent sobs.

"I can't—can't do anything for her. What good are hands as big as hams if they can't hold back the suffering she has to endure?"

They held on to each other through the longest hour

Gemma had ever known until the unit doors finally opened again.

The doctor stood in the doorway with a faint smile on his lips. "She is on a breathing machine and resting much easier now that the vent can do some of the work. The X-ray does show pneumonia in her right lower lung. We've started medication to help clear it, but I think she's going to be fine."

"Can we come in?" Jesse asked, wiping his eyes.

"Give the nurses another ten minutes to get things cleaned up. I don't recommend you hold her today. Let her rest after this. If she is doing okay tomorrow, I think it will be fine."

"*Danki,*" Gemma said.

The doctor nodded once and went back into the unit.

Gemma and Jesse stared at each other. Her relief was so profound she didn't know what to say.

He reached out and cupped her cheek. "I love you, Gemma. I think I've loved you since the day at the cabin when you knocked the cattail roots out of my hands and scolded me for getting frostbite."

She smiled softly. How could she have doubted this man? "I love you too."

They moved into each other's arms. Jesse kissed her forehead and held her tight. "I never want to let you go."

"That's fine with me, but I'm having a little trouble breathing." Her voice was muffled against his chest.

He chuckled as he loosened his hold. "Trust my Gemma to tell me what she thinks. I love that about you. I love everything about you." He drew a shaky breath. "I want to tell you about the land."

"You don't need to explain. I'm sorry I doubted your motives. I couldn't believe you wanted to marry me for myself alone. I didn't feel worthy of the sacrifice you were making. Jesse, I know in my heart that you are a man of integrity."

"Your father did offer me the land to marry you."

Her heart sank. "He did?"

"I refused and told him he didn't value the treasure he had in his daughter."

Her heart rebounded and thudded with joy. "I don't imagine he cared for that."

"I don't think he did, but he did give us the land as a wedding present. He said my farm wasn't big enough to raise a family on."

"I think it's a lovely farm. Although it is in need of some tender loving care."

He rested his forehead against hers. "You are worth far more to me than any amount of land in Maine."

She chuckled as all her doubts slipped away. "Of course I am. Farmland is dirt cheap up here. What would I be worth in Florida?"

"I believe the answer is in Proverbs 31:10. 'Who can find a virtuous woman? for her price is far above rubies.' Let's go in and see our daughter, shall we, my wife?"

"*Ja*, my husband."

Two and a half weeks later, Jesse opened the door to the suite where Gemma was staying. He'd gone back to New Covenant a week after Hope's recovery. He hadn't seen his wife or his daughter for a week. He dropped his duffel bag and held out his arms. Gemma rushed to hug him and gave him a quick peck on the cheek. "We have to get over to the nursery. The doctor wants a meeting with us."

"Now? I just got here. Can't I even say hello to you first?"

"Sorry." She raised her face for his kiss. It was still too brief before she pulled away, but it would have to do. "Come on. I want to find out what's going on."

"I thought you said she was getting well."

"She's been doing great. She weighs five pounds and seven ounces."

If his daughter was doing well, Jesse didn't understand what the rush was to see the doctor, but he hurried along beside his wife. In the unit, they were shown to a small office. The doctor came in a few seconds later. "Nice to see you again, Mr. Crump. I have some good news. Hope is ready to be discharged, and we need to make some going-home plans."

Discharged? They could take the baby home? Jesse glanced at Gemma. She was staring at the neonatologist like he was speaking Greek. Finally she said, "You mean Hope is well enough to go home? But she's so small."

"She is doing all the things we talked about. She is maintaining her temperature without heat. She is taking all her feedings and nursing well. And she is growing steadily. We can't do any better for her than you can."

Gemma clutched Jesse's arm. "It's too soon. We don't have anything ready for her at home."

The doctor grinned. "I suggest you get ready. She is going out the door on Monday morning."

On Monday afternoon, Dale Kaufman drove into the Lapp farm and stopped by the front gate. The farmyard was full of buggies and cars. "Looks like our new little gal has company already."

Jesse frowned. "The first thing they told us about taking her home was to avoid large crowds."

Gemma handed him the baby bundled up against the cold. "We can't stay in the car."

He took her hand and helped her out. The front door opened. Gemma's parents came out with Esther Hopper.

She stood back while Dinah and Leroy greeted the new arrival. Dinah took the baby from him and they all went into the house. It was empty.

Gemma looked around. "Where are the people who belong to the buggies outside?"

"In the barn," Leroy said, gazing fondly at the child.

Gemma and Jesse looked at each other. "What's going on?" he asked. "Why are people in the barn?"

"Because that's where it is warm enough to wait." Dinah smiled at Gemma. "Are you hungry? We have plenty of food."

Gemma cocked one eyebrow. "Do I have to go to the barn to get it?"

Dinah waved aside the question. "Of course not. I have some in the kitchen for you. I think we are ready to open gifts now. Esther, would you go tell the folks?"

"Gifts?" Jesse looked as puzzled as Gemma felt.

"This is your baby shower. Sit on the sofa with Hope so everyone can see her." She marshaled them to a place where the sofa had been turned to face the windows and opened the shades.

Esther went to the door. "She shouldn't be exposed to large crowds for a while, but everyone wants to see her."

Gemma's father pulled a cradle out from behind a chair. "Gemma, this cradle was made by your great-great-grandfather. I slept in it, as did you. May God grant you have many more children to rock to sleep in it."

"Now, my quilt," Dinah said. "This was made by myself and your cousins. By the way, there is a mud sale being planned in February by an Amish community in Ohio to raise funds for Hope's and Gemma's medical bills. We will have other fund-raisers soon. *Gott* provides."

One by one, the gifts from family and friends were displayed. There was a tap at the window. Gemma glanced up to see a dozen people lined up outside the windows, including the bishop, Mr. Meriwether, the grocer, Ivan and Jenny, their teachers and classmates from school, as well as Michael and Bethany. Everyone was bundled up against the cold. Bethany beckoned Gemma closer. Gemma handed the baby to Jesse. "Go show off your daughter."

He happily took Hope to the window and waited as guest after guest filed by to get a view of the newest resident of New Covenant. Gemma sat back and watched. She wouldn't say Jesse preened, but she had never seen him look so happy.

Two weeks after their arrival at her parents' home, Gemma and Hope were settling in well, except for one thing. Jesse had chosen to stay at his home until he had the place fixed up enough for his family to move there. While he came over every day, Gemma was wondering when she would be able to move into her new home.

She finished feeding Hope and was getting ready for bed on Saturday night when the sound of something hitting the window caught her attention. It sounded like a smattering of hail. She heard it again. What was going on?

She pulled up the shade. Jesse stood in the snow-covered garden below. A full moon hung low in the sky, making the scene almost as bright as day. She lifted the sash, letting in a rush of cold air. "Jesse Crump, what are you doing?"

"Dress warm and come out."

"Why?"

"Because I asked you to?"

"You will need a better explanation by the time I get down there."

"Come on. It's important."

She closed the window and quickly dressed. She pulled on long woolen leggings and put on her fur-lined boots. Hope was sound asleep in her bassinet beside her mother's bed.

Gemma tiptoed into her mother's room across the hall and gently shook her by the shoulder. "Mamm, wake up."

"What's wrong?" her mother whispered as she sat up.

"Nothing. Jesse wants me to come outside."

"At this time of night? What for?"

Gemma shrugged. "I have no idea. I left my door open. Will you listen for the baby?"

"Foolishness, if you ask me. Go, I'll keep an eye on her."

"Danki, Mamm." Gemma hurried down the hall to the front door, grabbed her coat and scarf from the peg and opened the door.

Jesse sat in a sleigh with one of his draft horses in harness.

Gemma came down the porch steps toward him. "What are you doing?"

"'Evening, Gemma."

She paused behind the gate. "Good evening to you. I don't understand."

"It's a right nice evening, isn't it?" His voice sounded strained.

"Nice enough for the dead of winter."

"I was wondering if you might like to take a sleigh ride?"

"Now?"

"That's how courting couples do it."

"Courting?" Her eyes widened.

"You never had a courtship. I thought you deserved one." Jesse held out his hand.

Gemma didn't hesitate. She pushed open the gate, took his hand and climbed in beside him. He spread a quilt over her lap. There were hot bricks on the floorboards to rest her feet on.

When she was settled beside him, he clicked his tongue and slapped the reins to set Goliath in motion.

At the highway, he turned south, away from the settlement. She couldn't contain her curiosity. "Where are we going?"

"Someplace we can talk without being interrupted."

"That could include ninety percent of the state of Maine." As if anyone was out and about at this time of night. He turned off on a road just beyond the Shultz place and then took the left fork behind their big white barn. The little-used road wound around the side of a hill and came out into a small meadow. A white-tailed buck stood browsing near the trees along the edge of the clearing. He bounded away in alarm.

Jesse drew his horse to a stop. "Will it bother you to walk a little ways?"

"I'll be fine."

"Not the *fine* word again."

"Okay. It won't bother me to walk."

"If you get tired or your ankle starts hurting, I'll carry you back to the sleigh."

She tucked that bit of information away to use later when she wanted to be held in his arms. At the moment, she was more curious about their destination.

Together, they walked side by side into the forest and down a faint path. The snow crunched under their boots. It wasn't long before she heard the sound of the water splashing over rocks. A few yards later, they came to an old stone bridge that spanned a rushing stream. They walked out into the middle of it, where Jesse stopped and leaned on the wall.

"How pretty it is here." Gemma stood beside him. The babbling of the water supplied the only sound. The air was motionless. The moon cast long shadows among the tall trees.

Jesse brushed the snow off the wall and sat on it. "I like to come here and think." He turned and pulled her to stand in front of him. He kept his arms around her and spoke softly in her ear. "Do you have any idea what kind of effect you have on me?"

"I hope that you view me as a dear friend." Her heart was beating so hard she feared he could hear it.

He smiled at her. "I don't think of you only as a friend."

He pulled off his gloves and cupped her face in his hands. "You and Hope have brought joy to me when I never expected to have it. I will never be able to thank God enough for bringing you into my life."

Before she could say anything, he bent his head and kissed her. His soft warm lips moved over hers, bringing a sensation of floating weightless in the night.

The sound of the rushing water faded away as Gemma tentatively explored the texture of his lips against hers. Firm but gentle, warm and tender, his touch sent the blood rushing through her veins. Softly, slowly, his lips moved to her cheeks and then to the side of her neck. She didn't know it was possible for her heart to expand with such love and not burst.

When Jesse drew away, she kept her eyes closed, afraid she would see disappointment or regret on his face.

"Gemma, look at me," he said softly.

"I can't."

Old insecurities came rushing back to choke down her happiness. "You must be ashamed of my behavior."

"Why would you say that?"

"Because you aren't the first man to kiss me in the moonlight."

"Gemma, I will tell you this only once. It doesn't matter who kissed you first. I will be the man who kisses you next and last and every day in between for the rest of our lives. I love you, Gemma."

She circled his neck with her arms. "My dear Jesse. I love you more than life itself. I think I truly fell in love with you when you lifted me out of Dale's pickup and held me in your arms. You were so incredibly strong and gentle at the same time."

"Does that mean I may court you? Nod if you agree."

She smiled at his teasing, even though she saw the

seriousness in his eyes. How was it possible to feel so happy?

"*Ja*, Jesse Crump, you may court me, but I warn you, I'm no great prize."

"I believe I get to be the judge of that." He nuzzled her cheek.

"How long will the courtship last?" She tipped her head so he could kiss her neck.

"Until the wedding."

"We're already married."

He drew back to grin at her. "Then there is no end in sight for us."

She rose onto her toes and kissed him with all the love she held in her heart for him.

He was the first to break away, drawing a deep unsteady breath that made her smile. He tucked her head beneath his chin. "I thought this was a romantic spot, but we should find somewhere warmer to continue our courting."

In the shadow of the trees, with the cold bright moonlight sparkling on the icy waters cascading below and his arms around her, Gemma had never been warmer in her life. "I'm fine."

"I'm happy for you, but my feet are freezing."

She chuckled. "You should have dressed warmer." He could always make her laugh. She loved that about him along with everything else.

He cupped her cheek with his hand. "I don't know why God chose this strange journey for you. From Maine to Florida and back just to end up in my arms."

"So that we'll never take each other for granted."

"That's what I think too." He bent and kissed her again.

She threaded her fingers through his hair and kept him close when he would have pulled away. "I plan to spend a lot of time kissing you, husband."

"*Goot*, for I plan to spend a little time kissing you back."

"Only a little?" She gave him a saucy grin.

He growled low in his throat. "God knew what he was doing when He brought you back into my life. I reckon He knew I needed someone to drive me crazy." He lowered his head to kiss her again.

Gemma melted against him as her heart was swept away by the love that flowed between her soul and his. Being courted by Jesse Crump surpassed all her expectations. God had been good to her.

* * * * *

If you enjoyed this story,
look for the first book in this series,
An Amish Wife for Christmas,
and Patricia Davids's new
The Amish of Cedar Grove *series*
from HQN Books:

The Wish
The Hope *(coming in December)*

Dear Reader,

I have once again taken you to Maine in the winter. I'm sorry. I promise a warmer time of the year to explore the beauty of New Covenant in my next book. Summer or spring? I haven't decided yet. I hope you enjoyed visiting some of the characters from my previous North Country Amish series. I'm always happy to let people catch up on the characters they wanted to know more about. There will be eight books in all set in Maine. I should be able to populate a small Amish community by then. If not, I can always keep going. That's the joy of my God-given gift. New ideas always pop into my head.

Blessings to you and yours,

Patricia Davids